FEATHERS, PAWS, FINS, AND CLAWS

SERIES IN FAIRY-TALE STUDIES

General Editor

Donald Haase, Wayne State University

Advisory Editors

Cristina Bacchilega, University of Hawai`i, Mānoa

Stephen Benson, University of East Anglia

Nancy L. Canepa, Dartmouth College

Anne E. Duggan, Wayne State University

Pauline Greenhill, University of Winnipeg

Christine A. Jones, University of Utah

Janet Langlois, Wayne State University

Ulrich Marzolph, University of Göttingen

Carolina Fernández Rodríguez, University of Oviedo

Maria Tatar, Harvard University

Jack Zipes, University of Minnesota

*A complete listing of the books in this series can
be found online at wsupress.wayne.edu*

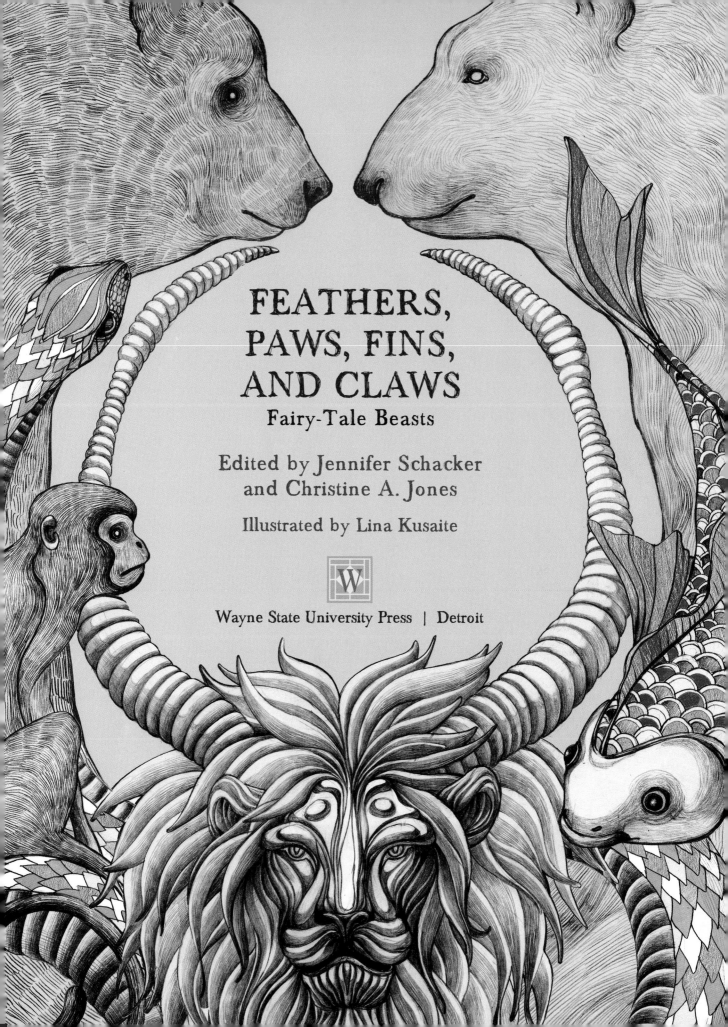

FEATHERS, PAWS, FINS, AND CLAWS

Fairy-Tale Beasts

Edited by Jennifer Schacker
and Christine A. Jones

Illustrated by Lina Kusaite

Wayne State University Press | Detroit

19 18 17 16 15   5 4 3 2 1

ISBN 978-0-8143-4069-1 (cloth)
ISBN 978-0-8143-4070-7 (e-book)

Library of Congress Control Number: 2014959210

∞

Designed and typeset by Bryce Schimanski
Composed in Adobe Caslon and Trade Gothic

For Jackson, Chloe, and Frida

CONTENTS

Editors' Note   ix

Introduction   1

Ballad of the Bird-Bride   19

The Story of the Three Bears   25

The Rat's Wedding   31

Babiole   41

Nanina's Sheep   69

Costantino Fortunato   77

East o' the Sun, West o' the Moon   83

The Snake-Skin   97

Prince Chéri   105

The Maiden and the Fish   119

EDITORS' NOTE

The stories in this volume are illustrated with original artwork by Lina Kusaite, inspired by the subtlety and richness of these historical texts. Nancy Canepa's translation of "Costantino Fortunato" is reprinted here with the generous permission of Broadview Press.

Where appropriate, antiquated spelling has been modernized by the editors, but in an effort to maintain the texture and character of each story, no other alterations have been made. For example, in "East o' the Sun, West o' the Moon," we have maintained the original placement of quotation marks around the heroine's reported or paraphrased speech. Although the outdated (and sometimes inconsistent) use of quotation marks in this tale may look odd, unconventional, or even incorrect to twenty-first-century readers, it marks the heroine's speech (and her declarations of her fearlessness) as noteworthy.

INTRODUCTION

A wide variety of creatures walk, fly, leap, slither, and swim through fairy-tale history. Some marvelous animal characters have taken up permanent residence in popular culture—the beast redeemed by beauty, the wolf in pursuit of little girls and little pigs, the frog prince released from enchantment by a young princess. Such fairy-tale animals may seem so familiar that they hardly require an introduction. But like the adventures of many fairy-tale heroes, the (re)reading of stories of these animal characters can yield surprises, challenges, and unexpected rewards.

While many North American readers have come to associate fairy tales with moral clarity, life lessons, and relatively fixed notions of gender, most narratives that make up fairy-tale history actually *resist* such characterizations. If contemporary readers can put aside their preconceptions about fairy tales, they are likely to discover a treasure trove of complicated stories that are morally ambiguous, frequently laced with irony and humor, and populated by characters who defy easy categorization in terms of class, gender, and even species!

For those of us who have grown up learning to read fairy tales in terms of locating the moral to each story, we can be lulled into a kind of complacency about what fairy tales are and the kinds of meanings they contain. It is just this complacency that fairy tales known as postmodern—whether short stories, novels, poetry, films, or television shows—attempt to disrupt. Recent reworkings of fairy-tale plots, characters, and motifs often blend what we have come to expect from tales (enchantment, moralism, and nostalgia) with the unexpected (weirdness, horror, and contemporary social concerns).[1] But one of the fascinating dimensions of fairy-tale history is that the impulses we associate with postmodern fairy tales actually have their roots in tales and texts from centuries ago. Indeed, if we reread historical tales with a new sense of wonder, we discover that they too delight in toying with our expectations and in this way invite us to see how uncanny the world can be. This is the kind of reading practice engaged in by curious, creative, and adventurous readers—whether they are exploring tales that are off the beaten track, such as the ones included in this book, or reconsidering fairy tales that are now mainstream. If familiarity makes fairy tales comfortable, then the older versions and obscure texts reproduced here may have an advantage over the currently popular ones in the practice of adventurous reading: they will surprise you with their candor and unexpected wit.

This volume of vintage tales was conceived especially for readers beyond childhood, those at an age when fairy tales may not appear to have much to offer and who therefore stand to be charmed by characters and plots they did not expect to find interesting. It can be disorienting to read tales that differ significantly from those fairy-tale favorites well known in North America today, and it can be equally challenging to rethink a familiar story in a fresh way—but both can be revealing and gratifying experiences. Before you begin your own exploration of the tales in this book, we invite you to consider with us one of the most widely known in twenty-first-century popular culture and featuring one of the most famous of all fairy-tale beasts: the story known as "Little Red Riding Hood." For the next few pages, we will focus on this case study to think about how we might *reread* fairy-tale beasts and rethink more general ideas about fairy tales.

At first glance, the role of the wolf in "Little Red Riding Hood" seems secondary: he represents an antagonistic element in the tale, the embodiment of evil. Indeed, in many popular versions of the story, the wolf appears as a dangerous stranger: he is a seducer, a predator, even a rapist/murderer—everything that a young girl should avoid in the world, represented as "wolf" because that predatory animal has cultural associations with solitude and cruelty. But when the wolf is placed in the company of a host of animal characters from fairy-tale history (such as those who populate the texts in *Feathers, Paws, Fins, and Claws*), we are invited to see him in a different light—perhaps even as the protagonist of the tale. Several contemporary writers have reimagined the story from the wolf's perspective.[2] Yet even if we look at a specific historical version of "Little Red Riding Hood" and peel away the presuppositions we bring to it, the story looks remarkably different than what we might expect, and its weirdness leaps to view.

Charles Perrault's French fairy tale "Le Petit Chaperon rouge" was the first print version of the story, published in 1697, and the one in which the heroine was officially named for the red clothing she wears. It is also the text on which countless English versions have been based. When we read the words in this 1697 French tale closely—whether in the original French or in an English translation—many striking and strange details present themselves that seem to *encourage* readers to see both the wolf and the heroine as complicated rather than flat, simple characters. We will focus momentarily on one word that concerns the introduction of the wolf as a character, and it is a word choice in French that has proven challenging for English translators: the narrator of the tale first introduces *le loup* (the wolf) not as big, bad, or nasty but as a *compère*. Now, you don't need to know French or to have read Perrault's original French text to sense that something interesting is afoot: in English translations, the phrase *compère le loup* is often rendered as "neighbor wolf" or, in older versions, "Gossop wolf." Both of these phrases undermine current assumptions about the wolf as representative of a dangerous stranger. The language of neighbor and the antiquated term "Gossop" (gossip) are suggestive of a friend, particularly a female friend. Close reading of a translation in which the wolf is introduced as a neighbor or (feminine) friend exposes layers of complexity in the story. Suddenly a so-called basic story for children looks much more interesting, and as professors we have had great fun watching students come to this realization.

But let's take a minute to think even more about the subtleties of the French phrase *compère le loup* to get a sense of just how tricky it is to translate into English.

In seventeenth-century French, the word *compère* would have had several meanings that are no longer part of the English definition of the term, making it an especially curious word choice. First and foremost, in the 1690s *compère* denoted a godfather, a social role that gives the wolf a spiritual relationship to the girl, as though he were present at her baptism. In this sense, he is (once again) not an outsider or a stranger or an outcast but instead is an intimate companion to people in the community. But there were other usages of the word circulating when Perrault chose to use it: in the 1690s, *compère* could also be used reciprocally, between a biological father and the man chosen to be godfather to his child. In this usage, the emphasis is on social and possibly spiritual bonds *between men*: each man was the other's *compère*, and they thus were linked by their relationship to each other (and to a child). In Perrault's rendition of this now well-known tale, the girl does not have a father, which makes the choice of the word very intriguing. What relationship *does* the wolf have to this girl? In what sense is he her *compère le loup*?

The third meaning circulating in the period complicates rather than clarifies: the term *compère* could be used to describe a man who looks out for his own self-interest and pleasure, who is passionate and alert (*fort éveillé, fort alerte*).[3] This definition later extends to the idea that a *compère* is a complicit friend, a partner in crime.[4] One strong thread runs through these definitions: all three suggest that a male figure deemed *compère* is, in one way or another, deeply embedded within the social fabric of a human community and knows how to operate in it. "Stranger danger" no longer sums up the perils faced by

Red Riding Hood—and, as a reader, you have some sense of just how far this kind of digging can go with the aid of a trusty dictionary.

Of course, the complexity of *compère* is not unique to this one word. Exploring the etymology and usages of any single word, in any language, can uncover multiple shades of meaning, usages that have fallen in and out of favor and ones that seem at odds with current usage. The seventeenth-century definitions of *compère* stand as just one particularly rich example, but similar and equally interesting explorations can focus on the multiple definitions and connotations of a word in specific translations of a given fairy tale. If you look up the word "gossip" you will find layers of possible meaning, and when you try them all out you will watch the wolf's personality transform before your eyes. The narrator in Perrault's "Le Petit Chaperon rouge" indeed seems to *invite* readers to dwell on *compère* (as we have done here), given that it is the one and only word used to introduce this particular wolf. So, how might knowledge about the word's potential meanings change the way we see the wolf?

First, it seems not at all strange for the girl to come upon and converse with a *compère* in the woods that separate her house and that of her grandmother. The girl would have no reason to fear such a godfatherly figure. But then again, the narrator points out in the next sentence that the girl "did not know that it is dangerous to stop and listen to a wolf" (*ne savait pas qu'il est dangereux de s'arrêter à écouter un loup*). Thus, even when he first appears, the wolf is both familiar and menacing to the girl, perhaps because he looks out for his own self-interest. He will retain this doubled personality, these seemingly contradictory traits, throughout the short tale.

Second, consider the paradox of a self-interested, predatory wolf that does not eat his prey right away. He uses his mouth to talk, civilly, rather than devour, animalistically. This is uncommon and is probably another invitation to take a closer look. The narrator notes that the wolf very much wanted to eat the girl but did not because there were "some woodcutters in the forest" (*quelques bûcherons dans la forêt*). Not simply motivated by physical appetite, this wolf understands the importance of appearances and perhaps of social contracts, as the primary definitions of *compère* suggest. Instead of gobbling up the girl on the spot he inquires about her trip, and she foolishly (the narrator points out) takes the bait. Yet she also buys herself all kinds of time—a fact of which she remains blissfully unaware. There are at least two subsequent moments after this initial escape from death when she could have opted not to move toward the wolf: she dallies in the forest and could have remained there in safety, among the woodcutters, and she could have flagged the problem when she arrived at her grandmother's house and "was at first afraid" of the deep voice she heard through the door. Instead, the girl quells her own anxiety with rationalization: she figures that her grandmother must be congested (*enhumée*). In other words, the girl convinces herself that she hears what she expected to hear—despite sensory evidence indicating something quite different.

The wolf's paradoxical nature emerges most fully in the final scene of the story when he interacts again with Red Riding Hood. When the girl arrives at the house and knocks, she hears a voice that seems strange. The wolf's voice is full (*grosse*) and deeper than her grandmother's but not so different that she doubts its veracity. This confusion of the wolf and the grandmother as separated *by degree* rather than type is significant, setting the stage for the climax and resolution of Perrault's story. Whatever felt animalistic about the wolf before now merges with the voice and body of the human grandmother. Perrault's title character follows the wolf/grandmother's directions without hesitation: she pulls the latch, opens the door, walks into the house, takes off her clothes—*se déshabille*—and crawls into the bed with the wolf/grandmother. It is only once in bed that the girl notices something odd: the wolf/grandmother is also *en son déshabillé*.

The image that has come down to us through translations, adaptations, and illustrations is that the wolf wears granny's nightclothes, but that isn't necessarily what the French suggests in this sentence, where a direct parallel is drawn between the girl's undressing and the state of undress in which she finds her grandmother. The noun used in French, *déshabillé*, comes from the past participle of *déshabiller*, meaning "to undress," and can refer to undergarments, sleepwear, or house clothes—the way one dresses at home, as opposed to the way one dresses to go out in public. Working with that definition, we might see how so many translators and illustrators have interpreted the image as one of a wolf who has *put on* the grandmother's nightgown or housecoat. Yet there is no indication in Perrault's text that the wolf undressed the grandmother before gobbling her up, nor is there any mention of him putting on any of her clothing. On the contrary, the feeding frenzy is quick enough that he must move from devouring the grandmother to impersonating her—almost instantaneously.

Since the narrator uses the verb *déshabiller* earlier in the same sentence when Red Riding Hood undresses, we might also see in the noun *son déshabillé* a more literal use of the term, meaning "completely undressed" or "naked." The use of the same root word draws a new parallel between the girl and the wolf/grandmother—both of whom are usually defined by their outermost layers, whether red hood or wolfish skin. Stripped down (literally and figuratively), Red Riding Hood begins to look different too. Within the span of a single sentence, Perrault has placed the two characters in the same bed and in a similar state of undress and vulnerability. In addition, the wolf and the grandmother are now so similar that the girl only registers the uncanniness of the creature next to her by degree: the arms, legs, ears, eyes, and teeth (all of which grandmother has too) are revealed to be remarkably "big." The enormous danger of the male wolf in this tale is not at all his strangeness but rather that he shares certain characteristics with female humans and hides in plain sight.

What comes out of this little romp through the forest with Little Red Riding Hood?

Like the wolf himself, familiar tales can become strange to us again when we consider each version of a tale in all its specificity and uniqueness. Giving a particular telling in history a close reading helps us embrace a story's ambiguities and uncertainties. In the case of animal tales, reading for ambiguity causes us to question broad claims about how animals have functioned in human cultures or in various historical periods. Moving from the specificity of Perrault's wolf to a broad spectrum of fairy-tale beasts, we can begin to see such characters as primary movers in the marvelous universe—ones that muddy the distinction and opposition of humans and animals.

Viewed in this light, Perrault's "Le Petit Chaperon rouge" can be seen as a cautionary tale—one not about strange men but about the act of reading itself. Both the tale's title character and the reader are in danger of overlooking what is right before their eyes: the wolf is both animal and human, both predatory and sociable, driven both by appetite and by calculated control of the situation. Above all, this wolf man is an intimately connected creature, both a *compère* and a grandmother, who bears little resemblance to the solitary, frightening, hairy-faced serial killer of werewolf lore. Without rethinking everything we have been told about Little Red Riding Hood, we might at first assume that Perrault's "Le Petit Chaperon rouge" is a story with a clear and uncontroversial message: don't talk to strangers. Certainly in the hands of tellers who have the goal of universal simplicity in mind, the story *could be* told in this way. But in Perrault's hands at the dawn of this wolf's fame, the story heightens ambiguity by turning the stranger into a cordial and conversant social animal.

To notice *this* personality in the beast, we just have to be open to hearing what is said, to seeing what is in front of us. Scratching the surface of even one word, one strange detail in the story, yields a whole host of considerations that we would not see if we did not spend time thinking about the wolf as a potentially multidimensional, complex character. By looking carefully at this and some other details from Perrault's French text, we want to emphasize, first, that *all* stories can be treated like archaeological sites: the more we dig, the more we find. Second, literary translation is both a science and an art. Every translator—no matter how dedicated he or she may be to accuracy—is a kind of storyteller, creating a new text rich with connotations and shades of meaning that may be quite different from the ones we find in the other language. The specific words chosen in a translated text will bring their own brand of complexity to a story and deserve just as much careful consideration as the words in William Shakespeare's plays or Jane Austen's novels.

Complexity is, in fact, a feature that fairy tales share with another genre well known for its beastly cast of characters: the fable. Both genres repeat recognizable, traditional plotlines, characters, and motifs in innumerable versions and variants—oral and written. Like fairy tales, fables seem to put simple stories in the service of clearly delivered moral messages. But as with fairy tales, the messages conveyed by any one basic storyline prove to be remarkably dynamic and unstable across the spectrum of re/tellings. To put it another way: the *potential* meanings and implications of a tale such as "Little Red Riding Hood" are many. Everything depends on the ways in which a particular tale is presented—the choices made by storytellers, writers, translators, illustrators, and editors. In the case of animal fables, such as those known in English literature as Aesop's fables, multiple and competing editions can include the "same" stories, and yet in their subtle and not-so-subtle differences, they can convey radically opposed messages and ideologies.[5] Stories are a lot more fun when we know to look for those differences.

Giving a timely tale the veneer of agedness and traditionality can grant a narrative a kind of unquestionable authority. To return to our case study, we can note that Perrault strategically deemed his own fairy tales *contes du temps passé* (tales of times past) while writing under the reign of Louis XIV and for a courtly audience well equipped to detect the subtleties of Perrault's socio-cultural references, such as those embedded in the phrase *compère le loup* or, say, the upstart strategies of a cat in boots. In traditional forms such as fairy tale and fable, each version, every retelling, has the ability to take a well-worn message or story and recast, reshape, or reconsider its implications for a new audience. In this sense, neither fables nor fairy tales are as universal as they can appear to be at first glance; in fact, their animal characters are open to endless reinterpretation.

When beasts inhabit stories as primary characters, they can play a wide variety of roles. As we hinted above, it is not the goal of this short collection to make broad claims about the role of animals in all folk narrative. The choice of tales you will encounter here has everything to do with idiosyncrasy rather than exemplarity and with diversity rather than comprehensiveness.[6] We have chosen texts from the literary history of fairy tales, such as "Costantino Fortunato" by the Renaissance Italian writer Giovan Francesco Straparola and "Babiole," written by Perrault's contemporary, Marie-Catherine d'Aulnoy. Inventive literary texts such as these already existed in dynamic interrelationship with local oral traditions, but the practice of documenting and analyzing orally told tales—what we would call folktales today—did not begin until the 1800s. Some of the stories in this volume are drawn from that history of folklore study, such as the Punjabi tale "The Rat's Wedding" and the Portuguese story "The Maiden and the Fish." Texts of this kind—collected from living storytellers, translated by professional scholars or amateur folklorists, and published as popular books in Victorian England—represent an important part of English fairy-tale history. Collections of oral tales from around the world provided new forms of inspiration for literary authors too, and Rosamund Marriott Watson's evocative poem "Ballad of the Bird-Bride," inspired by a collection of Inuit tales published in 1875, is one example of this phenomenon.[7] Each text included in *Feathers, Paws, Fins, and Claws* has its own history, summarized in our short introductions to individual stories. And each one of these narratives offers a unique snapshot into the various, sometimes comical ways beastly characters have appeared in fairy tales over the past two hundred years.

In this book we put animal tales in a new kind of context: an illustrated book for older readers that gathers material from a wide variety of traditions and textual sources and offers new visual interpretations by Belgian artist Lina Kusaite. The illustrator brings the full range of her creative virtuosity to bear upon the imaginative power of these tales. She belongs to a long line of artists who have illustrated collections of fairy tales for sophisticated readers, encouraging them to explore the subtleties and undercurrents that give each tale its personality.[8] Taken as a whole, the words and pictures in this book represent an international collaboration (Canada, the United States, Belgium) that brings together insights from the fields of folklore and literary studies, French history and British popular culture, and fantasy and design history.

Kusaite's illustrations certainly serve to beautify the book, but more than that they represent concrete examples of how creative interpretation can make us think very differently about stories that could appear facile or (on the surface) easily understood. We welcome you to interrogate this wild and motley bestiary—in the highly creative manner that Kusaite does—and discover how particular animals look to you and how they operate, both as individuals in particular stories and as a group of creatures whose behaviors span the full range of human and nonhuman possibility.

Of the ten stories included here, seven are translations from other languages, and all but one of those translations are over one hundred years old. As this volume attests, fairy tales and translation go hand in hand. As has now become evident, fairy tales are made primarily from recycled material—a very "sustainable" type of writing!—and like handcraft-

have made only very small changes to historical spelling and punctuation in order to retain the vintage patina of the writing. The forms you will encounter in this book range from literary ballad to tales long enough to be called short stories. Our beasts move between what we might see as typical animal behavior (a bird seeking to spread its wings and fly or a clever cat artfully catching its prey) and acts that seem much more human than beastly (three fastidious bears keeping a tidy home together, for example, or a snake inviting itself to the dinner table). The drama of these tales emerges as we watch humans and animals in interspecies conflict. And sometimes the same character shape-shifts across identities, giving him or her particular insight into the nature of how individual creatures interact with each other. In short, we chose a group of narratives that employ animals to different ends: four follow the familiar fairy-tale convention of the cursed prince or princess that takes an animal form temporarily ("Babiole," "East o' the Sun, West o' the Moon," "The Snake-Skin," and "The Maiden and the Fish"), five feature animals playing themselves with a variety of human qualities ("Ballad of the Bird-Bride," "The Story of the Three Bears," "The Rat's Wedding," "Nanina's Sheep," and "Costantino Fortunato"), and one showcases both tendencies ("Prince Chéri"). All of the extraordinary animals in these fairy tales flout conventional stereotypes about their motivations and desires. They can make us more aware of what it is *to be* human—or to be a good human being—but they also help us to think critically about our relationships with the rest of the animal kingdom.

Finally, as we have suggested here, our own scholarly investigations of the fairy-tale past cause us to resist broad claims about the role of animals in certain periods or in human history; on the contrary, we delight—and hope you will too—in the way in which such generalizations become harder and harder to make the more closely we read individual stories and specific fairy-tale characters. We welcome the reader to enter this bestiary and discover how these particular animals look and operate, to let these older fairy tales work on our modern imaginations now. This is the very same spirit that motivates Lina Kusaite in the artwork she crafted for this book. Her evocative images invite expansive responses, in the spirit of fairy-tale history itself. Every fairy-tale text leaves open the possibility of innumerable other versions, told and waiting to be told by innumerable creative storytellers—perhaps by you.

Jennifer Schacker and Christine A. Jones

Notes

1. Recent critical studies of fairy tales in contemporary literature, film, and other media include the essays in Pauline Greenhill and Jill Terry Rudy, eds., *Channeling Wonder: Fairy Tales on Television* (Detroit: Wayne State UP, 2014); Cristina Bacchilega, *Fairy Tales Transformed? Twenty-First Century Adaptations and the Politics of Wonder* (Detroit: Wayne State UP, 2013); and Jack Zipes, *The Enchanted Screen: The Unknown History of Fairy-Tale Films* (New York: Routledge, 2010). For an anthology of contemporary fiction concerning fairy-tale animals, see Ellen Datlow and Terri Windling, eds., *The Beastly Bride: Tales of the Animal People* (New York: Viking, 2010).

2. Several twentieth- and twenty-first-century tales that foreground the character of the wolf have been collected by one of the premier scholars of Little Red Riding Hood, Sandra Beckett; see her recent collection *Revisioning Red Riding Hood around the World: An Anthology of International Readings* (Detroit: Wayne State UP, 2014), especially chapters 4 and 5.

3. "Compere," *Dictionnaire de l'Académie Française* (1697), ARTFL Project, Web, May 23, 2014. Note that the modern French word has an accent (*compère*), but the seventeenth-century spelling does not use it.

4. Jean-Pierre Collinet and Martine Hennard have noted that this meaning of the word can be traced to Jean de La Fontaine's fables, where characters, in particular the fox, have or solicit a *compère*, a friend/partner to help them do their (sometimes dirty) work. Jean-Pierre Collinet, ed., *Perrault Contes* (Paris: Folio classique, 1999), 70, note 4. Martine Hennard Dutheil de la Rochère, "Updating the Politics of Experience: Angela Carter's Translation of Charles Perrault's 'Le Petit Chaperon rouge,'" *Palimpsestes* 22 (2009): 4, Web, May 23, 2014. See also Henri Régnier's *Œuvres de J. de La Fontaine: Lexique de la*

langue, Vol. 10 (Paris: Hachette, 1892), 177, which tracks appearances of the word *compère* in La Fontaine's fables.

5. It is no accident that the genre of the fable flourished during periods of extreme political and social instability, such as the years of the English Civil War, when writers across the political spectrum drew on this ancient form to explore timely questions about human rights, power, and forms of authority. On the political uses of animal fables, see Annabel Patterson, *Fables of Power: Aesopian Writing and Political History* (Durham, NC: Duke UP, 1991), and Jayne Elizabeth Lewis, *The English Fable: Aesop and Literary Culture, 1651–1740* (Cambridge: Cambridge UP, 1996).

6. The present volume draws on a recent critical tendency to think about animal-human hybridity in specifically cultural terms. For example, Suzanne Magnanini explores the monsters of late Italian Renaissance fairy tales (ca. 1550–1625) in terms of historical developments in science. See *Fairy-Tale Science: Monstrous Generation in the Tales of Straparola and Basile* (Toronto: U of Toronto P, 2008).

7. Nineteenth-century England represents one of the most fertile places and periods in fairy-tale history. An enormous number of tale collections (folkloristic and literary) were composed, translated, or reprinted in the Victorian period, and references to fairy tales abounded in a wide variety of communicative forms, such as novels, poetry, advertisements, theatrical performances, political tracts, and the visual arts. On the complex relationship between the genre and Victorian ideas about modernity, see Molly Clark Hillard, *Spellbound: The Fairy Tale and the Victorians* (Columbus: Ohio State UP, 2014); on the emergence of the field-based tale collection as popular reading material, see Jennifer Schacker, *National Dreams: The Remaking of Fairy Tales in Nineteenth-Century England* (Philadelphia: U of Pennsylvania P, 2003); on the relationship between colonialism and British folklore study, see Sadhana Naithani, *The Story-Time of the British Empire: Colonial and Postcolonial Folkloristics* (Jackson: UP of Mississippi, 2010).

8. Among the exemplary visual interpretations that punctuate fairy-tale history are the nineteenth-century illustrations of Perrault's tales by Gustave Doré in *Les Contes de Charles Perrault* (Paris: Hetzel, 1867). These ubiquitous images are now known the world over and have been enormously influential on the contemporary sense of Perrault's tales (such as the wolf in the grandmother's bonnet).

9. According to the *Dictionnaire de l'Académie Française* of 1694, the word *chaperon* refers to a medieval and Renaissance style of headpiece with a tufted top and a kind of fabric tail that falls down onto the shoulders. Samber's association of the headpiece with horseback-riding gear results from a creative combination of etymologies. The French word

chaperon is a diminutive of *chape*, whose first definition is a long robe worn by the clergy: a cassock. The word "cassock" was used in seventeenth-century England to refer to the long cloak that horsemen wore (Oxford English Dictionary). Thus, Samber combined *chaperon*, or little riding cloak, with the idea of a head covering to yield "riding hood."

10. Andrew Teverson's introduction to *Fairy Tales* (Abingdon, UK: Routledge/New Critical Idiom, 2013) does a fine job of capturing the slipperiness of fairy tales, a genre he characterizes as derivative, deeply layered with history, and highly interpretable (3–4). Ultimately, he invites readers to find in them, as we have suggested here, a "receptacle of cultural preoccupations that is forever being reinvented" (7).

BALLAD OF THE BIRD-BRIDE

The power, freedom, and beauty of birds in flight have had a kind of magical hold on the human imagination for millennia. In this haunting ballad by the Victorian poet Rosamund Marriott Watson, an earthbound man laments the loss of his wife—a bird-woman whose true nature could be neither contained, suppressed, nor transformed by marriage. Watson attributes the source of "Ballad of the Bird-Bride" to "the Eskimo"; in fact, an 1875 volume of Greenland Inuit tales and traditions collected by Hinrich Johannes (Henry) Rink was a popular book in England and includes Watson's likely inspiration, "The Man Who Mated Himself with a Sea-Fowl." As in Celtic and north European stories of selkies (seal women), marriage in this fairy tale brings discontent and sorrow, not a happy ending. The lure of the skies for the bird-bride proves far stronger than the bonds of marriage—a rich thematic for Watson as a woman writer publishing under a male pseudonym (a variant of her second husband's name)—whose personal life challenged conventional Victorian morality, ultimately leading to the social ostracization of this once prominent poet and salon hostess. In this poem Watson adopts the voice of the abandoned husband, drawing on many of the formal and stylistic conventions of traditional British ballads. Today there are perhaps many ways we can understand the bird-woman's need to take flight from an existence she did not choose, a domestic life that kept her captive, and a loving man who nonetheless wanted to tame her. At the same time, Watson seems to invite us to empathize with the man who has lost both his wife and his children.

"Ballad of the Bird-Bride," in Graham R. Tomson [Rosamund Marriott Watson], *The Bird-Bride: A Volume of Ballads and Sonnets* (New York: Longmans, Green, 1889), 1–5.

(Eskimo)

They never come back, though I loved them well;
    I watch the South in vain;
The snow-bound skies are blear and grey,
Waste and wide is the wild gull's way,
    And she comes never again.

Years agone, on the flat white strand,
    I won my sweet sea-girl:
Wrapped in my coat of the snow-white fur,
I watched the wild birds settle and stir,
    The grey gulls gather and whirl.

One, the greatest of all the flock,
    Perched on an ice-floe bare,
Called and cried as her heart were broke,
And straight they were changed, that fleet bird-folk,
    To women young and fair.

Swift I sprang from my hiding-place
    And held the fairest fast;
I held her fast, the sweet, strange thing:
Her comrades skirled, but they all took wing,
    And smote me as they passed.

I bore her safe to my warm snow house;
    Full sweetly there she smiled;
And yet, whenever the shrill winds blew,
She would beat her long white arms anew,
    And her eyes glanced quick and wild.

But I took her to wife, and clothed her warm
　　With skins of the gleaming seal;
Her wandering glances sank to rest
When she held a babe to her fair, warm breast,
　　And she loved me dear and leal.

Together we tracked the fox and the seal,
　　And at her behest I swore
That bird and beast my bow might slay
For meat and for raiment, day by day,
　　But never a grey gull more.

A weariful watch I keep for aye
　　'Mid the snow and the changeless frost:
Woe is me for my broken word!
Woe, woe's me for my bonny bird,
　　My bird and the love-time lost!

Have ye forgotten the old keen life?
　　The hut with the skin-strewn floor?
O winged white wife, and children three,
Is there no room left in your hearts for me,
　　Or our home on the low sea-shore?

Once the quarry was scarce and shy,
　　Sharp hunger gnawed us sore,
My spoken oath was clean forgot,
My bow twanged thrice with a swift, straight shot,
　　And slew me sea-gulls four.

The sun hung red on the sky's dull breast,
  The snow was wet and red;
Her voice shrilled out in a woeful cry,
She beat her long white arms on high,
  "The hour is here," she said.

She beat her arms, and she cried full fain
  As she swayed and wavered there.
"Fetch me the feathers, my children three,
Feathers and plumes for you and me,
  Bonny grey wings to wear!"

They ran to her side, our children three,
  With the plumage black and grey;
Then she bent her down and drew them near,
She laid the plumes on our children dear,
  'Mid the snow and the salt sea-spray.

"Babes of mine, of the wild wind's kin,
  Feather ye quick, nor stay.
Oh, oho! but the wild winds blow!
Babes of mine, it is time to go:
  Up, dear hearts, and away!"

And lo! the grey plumes covered them all,
  Shoulder and breast and brow.
I felt the wind of their whirling flight:
Was it sea or sky? was it day or night?
  It is always night-time now.

Dear, will you never relent, come back?
 I loved you long and true.
O winged white wife, and our children three,
Of the wild wind's kin though ye surely be,
 Are ye not of my kin too?

Ay, ye once were mine, and, till I forget,
 Ye are mine forever and aye,
Mine, wherever your wild wings go,
While shrill winds whistle across the snow
 And the skies are blear and grey.

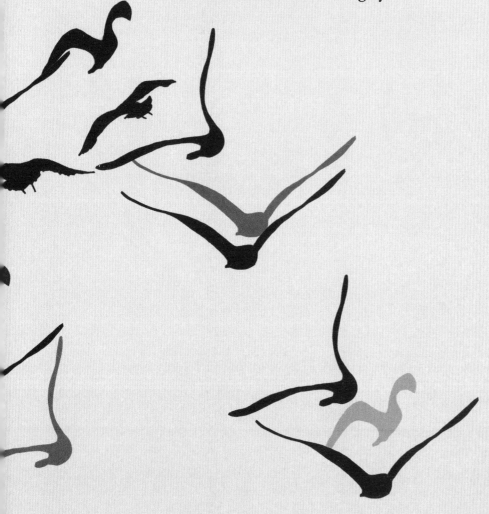

THE STORY OF
THE THREE BEARS

The story of three porridge-loving bears who live in a little house in the woods is a classic of modern children's literature, but it has changed pretty dramatically from the form in which it was first published by British Romantic poet Robert Southey in 1834. Modern readers can be surprised to discover that there is no golden-haired little girl in "The Story of the Three Bears." Before the introduction of Goldilocks, the story concerned the invasion of the bears' house by a vagrant old woman—driven by her appetites, unconcerned with social norms and mores—who leaves chaos and destruction in her wake. This version of the story continued to be printed through the nineteenth century (the one included here is from Joseph Jacobs's 1890 English Fairy Tales*). And while some readers may expect the story to operate as a lesson in etiquette for children (Don't trespass! Don't make yourself at home unless invited to do so!), in this earlier form the fairy tale's appeal seems unruly, transgressive, and broadly humorous. The bears themselves—three males of varying sizes—keep a very tidy, orderly, and respectable home by human standards. So, who exactly is the wild animal in this fairy tale?*

Once upon a time there were Three Bears, who lived together in a house of their own, in a wood. One of them was a Little, Small Wee Bear; and one was a Middle-sized Bear, and the other was a Great, Huge Bear. They had each a pot for their porridge, a little pot for the Little, Small, Wee Bear; and a middle-sized pot

"The Story of the Three Bears," in Joseph Jacobs, *English Fairy Tales* (London: David Nutt, 1890), 93–98.

for the Middle Bear, and a great pot for the Great, Huge Bear. And they had each a chair to sit in; a little chair for the Little, Small, Wee Bear; and a middle-sized chair for the Middle Bear; and a great chair for the Great, Huge Bear. And they had each a bed to sleep in; a little bed for the Little, Small, Wee Bear; and a middle-sized bed for the Middle Bear; and a great bed for the Great, Huge Bear.

One day, after they had made the porridge for their breakfast, and poured it into their porridge-pots, they walked out into the wood while the porridge was cooling, that they might not burn their mouths, by beginning too soon to eat it. And while they were walking, a little old Woman came to the house. She could not have been a good, honest old Woman; for first she looked in at the window, and then she peeped in at the keyhole; and seeing nobody in the house, she lifted the latch. The door was not fastened, because the Bears were good Bears, who did nobody any harm, and never suspected that anybody would harm them. So the little old Woman opened the door, and went in; and well pleased she was when she saw the porridge on the table. If she had been a good little old Woman, she would have waited till the Bears came home, and then, perhaps, they would have asked her to breakfast; for they were good Bears—a little rough or so, as the manner of Bears is, but for all that very good-natured and hospitable. But she was an impudent, bad old Woman, and set about helping herself.

So first she tasted the porridge of the Great, Huge Bear, and that was too hot for her; and she said a bad word about that. And then she tasted the porridge of the Middle Bear, and that was too cold for her; and she said a bad word about that too. And then she went to the porridge of the Little, Small, Wee Bear, and tasted that; and that was neither too hot, nor too cold, but just right; and she liked it so well, that she ate it all up: but the naughty old Woman said a bad word about the little porridge-pot, because it did not hold enough for her.

Then the little old Woman sat down in the chair of the Great, Huge Bear, and that was too hard for her. And then she sat down in the chair of the Middle Bear, and that was too soft for her. And then she sat down in the chair of the Little, Small, Wee Bear, and that was neither too hard, nor too soft, but just right. So she seated herself in it, and there she sat till the bottom of the chair came out, and down she came, plump upon the ground. And the naughty old Woman said a wicked word about that too.

Then the little old Woman went upstairs into the bedchamber in which the three Bears slept. And first she lay down upon the bed of the Great, Huge Bear; but that was too high at the head for her. And next she lay down upon the bed of the Middle Bear; and that was too high at the foot for her. And then she lay down upon the bed of the Little, Small, Wee Bear; and that was neither too high at the head, nor at the foot, but just right. So she covered herself up comfortably, and lay there till she fell fast asleep.

By this time the Three Bears thought their porridge would be cool enough; so they came home to breakfast. Now the little old Woman had left the spoon of the Great, Huge Bear, standing in his porridge.

"Somebody has been at my porridge!"

said the Great, Huge Bear, in his great, rough, gruff voice. And when the Middle Bear looked at his, he saw that the spoon was standing in it too. They were wooden spoons; if they had been silver ones, the naughty old Woman would have put them in her pocket.

"Somebody has been at my porridge!"

said the Middle Bear in his middle voice.

Then the Little, Small, Wee Bear looked at his, and there was the spoon in the porridge-pot, but the porridge was all gone.

*"Somebody has been at my porridge,
and has eaten it all up!"*

said the Little, Small, Wee Bear, in his little, small, wee voice.

Upon this the Three Bears, seeing that some one had entered their house, and eaten up the Little, Small, Wee Bear's breakfast, began to look about them. Now the little old Woman had not put the hard cushion straight when she rose from the chair of the Great, Huge Bear.

"Somebody has been sitting in my chair!"

said the Great, Huge Bear, in his great, rough, gruff voice.

And the little old Woman had squatted down the soft cushion of the Middle Bear.

"Somebody has been sitting in my chair!"

said the Middle Bear, in his middle voice.

And you know what the little old Woman had done to the third chair.

*"Somebody has been sitting in my chair
and has sat the bottom out of it!"*

said the Little, Small, Wee Bear, in his little, small, wee voice.

Then the Three Bears thought it necessary that they should make farther search; so they went upstairs into their bedchamber. Now the little old Woman had pulled the pillow of the Great, Huge Bear, out of its place.

"Somebody has been lying in my bed!"

said the Great, Huge Bear, in his great, rough, gruff voice.

And the little old Woman had pulled the bolster of the Middle Bear out of its place.

"Somebody has been lying in my bed!"

said the Middle Bear, in his middle voice.

And when the Little, Small, Wee Bear came to look at his bed, there was the bolster in its place; and the pillow in its place upon the bolster; and upon the pillow was the little old Woman's ugly, dirty head,—which was not in its place, for she had no business there.

"Somebody has been lying in my bed,—and here she is!"

said the Little, Small, Wee Bear, in his little, small, wee voice.

The little old Woman had heard in her sleep the great, rough, gruff voice of the Great, Huge Bear; but she was so fast asleep that it was no more to her than the roaring of wind, or the rumbling of thunder. And she had heard the middle voice, of the Middle Bear, but it was only as if she had heard some one speaking in a dream. But when she heard the little, small, wee voice of the Little, Small, Wee Bear, it was so sharp, and so shrill, that it awakened her at once. Up she started and when she saw the Three Bears on one side of the bed, she tumbled herself out at the other, and ran to the window. Now the window was open, because the Bears, like good, tidy Bears, as they were, always opened their bedchamber window when they got up in the morning. Out the little old Woman jumped; and whether she broke her neck in the fall; or ran into the wood and was lost there; or found her way out of the wood, and was taken up by the constable and sent to the House of Correction for a vagrant as she was, I cannot tell. But the Three Bears never saw anything more of her.

THE RAT'S WEDDING

Known on the modern urban landscape as ruthless scavengers, household pests, parasites, or carriers of disease, rats have also been associated with a more positive characteristic: cleverness. The rat at the center of this South Asian tale makes a series of rather canny bargains with human beings, his ambitions, rewards, and confidence growing with each exchange he makes. However, when the rat trades a buffalo for a princess bride, the irony of the story's title becomes clear. The rat sees the young woman as an object of exchange, but the deep misogyny implicit in his actions is exposed and undermined by none other than her mother, the queen. Playing to the rat's ego and unfettered desires, the queen manages to free her daughter and send the rat scurrying away, singed and humiliated, vowing to avoid future bargaining. In its present form, this story was introduced to English-language readers in 1884 by the English writer and tale collector Flora Annie Steel. Steel worked in collaboration with Richard Temple, an officer in the British Indian Army and editor of the monthly folklore periodical The Indian Antiquary, in which many oral stories collected by Steel and annotated by Temple first appeared. In Wide-Awake Stories, Steel and Temple edited and recast a selection of stories, trying to address the taste and expectations of "the little Reader" but still including lengthy scholarly notes. One has to wonder how far removed this printed text is from the tale Steel heard narrated over a century ago in northern India, but today's readers can still delight in this story of a clever rodent who tries to make one bargain too many and of smart and resourceful women who triumph over a male "rat."

"The Rat's Wedding," in F. A. Steel and R. C. Temple, *Wide-Awake Stories: A Collection of Tales Told by Little Children, between Sunset and Sunrise, in the Punjab and Kashmir* (Bombay: Education Society's Press, 1884), 17–26.

Once upon a time a fat sleek Rat was caught in a shower of rain, and being far from shelter he set to work and soon dug a nice hole in the ground, in which he sat as dry as a bone while the rain-drops splashed outside, making little puddles on the road.

Now in the course of his digging he came upon a fine bit of root, quite dry and fit for fuel, which he set aside carefully—for the Rat is an economical creature—in order to take it home with him. So when the shower was over, he set off with the dry root in his mouth. As he went along, daintily picking his way through the puddles, he saw a poor man vainly trying to light a fire, while a little circle of children stood by, and howled.

"Goodness gracious!" cried the Rat, who was both soft-hearted and curious, "what a dreadful noise to make! What *is* the matter?"

"The bairns are hungry," answered the man; "they are crying for their breakfast, but the sticks are damp, the fire won't burn, so I can't bake the cakes."

"If that is all your trouble, perhaps I can help you," said the goodnatured Rat; "you are welcome to this dry root, and I'll warrant it will soon make a fine blaze."

The poor man with a thousand thanks took the dry root, and in his turn presented the Rat with a morsel of dough, as a reward for his kindness and generosity.

"What a remarkably lucky fellow I am!" thought the Rat, as he trotted off gaily with his prize, "and clever too! Fancy making a bargain like that—food enough to last me five days in return for a rotten old stick! Wah! wah! wah! What it is to have brains!"

Going along, hugging his good fortune in this way, he came presently to a potter's yard, where the potter, leaving his wheel to spin round by itself, was trying to pacify his three little children, who were howling, screaming, and crying, as if they would burst.

"My gracious!" cried the Rat, stopping his ears, "what a row!—do tell me what it is all about."

"I suppose they are hungry," replied the potter ruefully; "their mother has gone to get flour in the bazaar, for there is none in the house. In the mean time I can neither work nor rest because of the noise."

"Is that all!" answered the officious Rat; "then I can help you. Take this dough, cook it quickly, and stop their mouths."

The potter overwhelmed the Rat with thanks for his obliging kindness, and choosing out a nice well-burnt pipkin, insisted on his accepting it as a remembrance.

The Rat was delighted at the exchange, and though the pipkin was just a trifle awkward to manage, he succeeded after infinite trouble in balancing it on his head, and went away gingerly, tink-a-tink, tink-a-tink, down the road, with his tail over his arm for fear he should trip on it. And all the time he kept saying to himself, "What a lucky fellow I am! and clever too! Such a hand at a bargain!"

By-and-bye he came to where some neatherds were herding their cattle. One of them was milking a buffalo, and having no pail he used his shoes instead.

"Oh fie! oh fie!" cried the cleanly Rat, quite shocked at the sight. "What a nasty dirty trick!—why don't you use a pail?"

"For the best of all reasons—we haven't got one!" growled the neatherd, who didn't see why the Rat should put his finger in the pie.

"If that is all," replied the dainty Rat, "oblige me by using this pipkin, for I can't bear dirt!"

The neatherd, nothing loth, took the pipkin, and milked away until it was brimming over; then turning to the Rat, who stood looking on, said, "Here, little fellow, you may have a drink, in payment."

But if the Rat was good natured he was also shrewd. "No, no, my friend," said he, "none of that! As if I could drink the worth of my pipkin at a draught!

My dear sir, *I couldn't hold it!* Besides, I never make a bad bargain, and I expect you to give me the buffalo."

"Rubbish!" cried the neatherd; "a buffalo for a pipkin! Who ever heard of such a price? And what on earth could you do with the big brute when you got it?—the pipkin was about as much as you could manage."

At this the Rat drew himself up with dignity; he did not like allusions to his size.

"That is my affair, not yours," be retorted; "your business is to hand over the buffalo."

So just for the fun of the thing, and to amuse themselves at the Rat's expense, the neatherds loosed the buffalo's halter and began to tie it to the little animal's tail.

"Hi! ho!" he shouted, in a great hurry; "why, if the beast pulled, the skin of my tail would come off, and then where should I be? Tie it round my neck, if you please."

So with much laughter the neatherds tied the halter round the Rat's neck, and he, after a polite leave-taking, set off gaily towards home with his prize,—that is to say, he set off with the *rope*, for no sooner did he come to the end of the tether than he was brought up with a round turn. The buffalo, nose down, would not budge until it had finished its tuft of grass; and then, seeing another in a different direction, marched off towards it, while the Rat, to avoid being dragged, had to trot humbly behind, willy nilly.

He was too proud to confess it, of course, and, nodding his head knowingly to the neatherds, said, "Ta-ta, good people! I am going home this way. It may be a little longer, but it's much shadier."

And when the neatherds roared with laughter he took no notice, but trotted on, looking as dignified as possible.

"After all," he reasoned to himself, "when one keeps a buffalo one has to look after its grazing. A beast must get a good bellyful of grass if it is to give any milk, and I have plenty of time at my disposal."

So all day long he trotted about after the buffalo, making believe; but by evening he was dead beat, and truly thankful when the great big beast, having eaten enough, lay down under a tree to chew the cud.

Just then a bridal party came by. The bridegroom and his friends had evidently gone on to the next village, leaving the bride's palanquin to follow; so the palanquin bearers, being lazy fellows, and seeing a nice shady tree, put down their burden, and began to cook some food.

"What detestable meanness!" grumbled one; "a grand wedding, and nothing but plain pulau to eat! Not a scrap of meat in it, neither sweet nor salt! It would serve the skinflints right if we upset the bride in a ditch!"

"Dear me!" cried the Rat at once, "that is a shame! I sympathise with your feelings so entirely, that if you will allow me I'll give you my buffalo. You can kill it, and cook it."

"*Your* buffalo!" returned the discontented bearers, "what rubbish! Whoever heard of a rat owning a buffalo?"

"Not often, I admit," replied the Rat with conscious pride; "but look for yourselves. Can you not see I am leading the beast by a string?"

"Bother the string!" cried a great big hungry bearer; "master or no master, I'll have meat to my dinner!"

Whereupon they killed the buffalo, and, cooking its flesh, ate their pulau with relish; then, offering the remains to the Rat, said carelessly, "Here, little Rat-skin, that is for you!"

"Now look here!" cried the Rat hotly; "I'll have none of your pulau, nor your sauce either. You don't suppose I am going to give my best buffalo, that gave quarts and quarts of milk—my buffalo I have been feeding all day—for a wee bit of pulau? No!—I got a loaf for a bit of stick; I got a pipkin for a little loaf; I got a buffalo for a pipkin; and now have the bride for my buffalo—the bride, and nothing else!"

By this time the servants, having satisfied their hunger, began to reflect on what they had done, and becoming alarmed at the consequences, arrived at the conclusion it would be wisest to make their escape whilst they could. So, leaving the bride in her palanquin, they took to their heels in various directions.

The Rat, being as it were left in possession, advanced to the palanquin, and drawing aside the curtain, with the sweetest of voices and best of bows begged the bride to descend. She hardly knew whether to laugh or to cry, but as any company, even a Rat's, was better than being quite alone in the wilderness, she did as she was bidden, and followed the lead of her guide, who set off as fast as he could for his hole.

As he trotted along beside the lovely young bride, who, by her rich dress and glittering jewels seemed to be some king's daughter, he kept saying to himself "How clever I am! What bargains I do make, to be sure!"

When they arrived at his hole, the Rat stepped forward with the greatest politeness, and said, "Welcome, Madam, to my humble abode! Pray step in, or if you will allow me, and as the passage is somewhat dark, I will show you the way."

Whereupon he ran in first, but after a time, finding the bride did not follow, he put his nose out again, saying testily, "Well, Madam, why don't you follow? Don't you know it's rude to keep your husband waiting?"

"My good sir," laughed the handsome young bride, "I can't squeeze into that little hole!"

The Rat coughed; then after a moment's thought he replied, "There is some truth in your remark—you *are* overgrown, and I suppose I shall have to build you a thatch somewhere. For tonight you can rest under that wild plum-tree."

"But I am so hungry!" said the bride, ruefully.

"Dear, dear! Everybody seems hungry today!" returned the Rat pettishly; "however, that's easily settled,—I'll fetch you some supper in a trice!"

So he ran into his hole, returning immediately with an ear of millet and a dry pea.

"There!" said he, triumphantly, "isn't that a fine meal?"

"I can't eat that!" whimpered the bride; "it isn't a mouthful; and I want pulau, and cakes, and sweet eggs, and sugar-drops. I shall die if I don't get them!"

"Oh, bother!" cried the Rat in a rage, "what a nuisance a bride is, to be sure! Why don't you eat the wild plums?"

"I can't live on wild plums!" retorted the weeping bride; "nobody could; besides, they are only half ripe, and I can't reach them."

"Rubbish!" cried the Rat; "ripe or unripe, they must do for you tonight, and tomorrow you can gather a basketful, sell them in the city, and buy sugar-drops and sweet eggs to your heart's content!"

So the next morning the Rat climbed up into the plum-tree, and nibbled away at the stalks till the fruit fell down into the bride's veil. Then, unripe as they were, she carried them into the city, calling out through the streets—

"Green plums I sell! green plums I sell!
Princess am I, Rat's bride as well!"

As she passed by the palace, her mother the Queen heard her voice, and, running out, recognised her daughter. Great were the rejoicings, for everyone thought the poor bride had been eaten by wild beasts. In the midst of the feasting and merriment, the Rat, who had followed the Princess at a distance, and had become alarmed at her long absence, arrived at the door, against which he beat with a big knobby stick, calling out fiercely, "Give me my wife! give me my wife! She is mine by fair bargain. I gave a stick and I got a loaf; I gave a loaf and I got a pipkin; I gave pipkin and I got a buffalo; I gave a buffalo and I got a bride. Give me my wife! give me my wife!"

"La! son-in-law! what a *fuss* you do make!" said the wily old Queen, through the door, "and all about nothing! Who wants to run away with your wife? On the contrary, we are proud to see you, and I only keep you waiting at the door till we can spread the carpets, and receive you in style."

Hearing this, the Rat was mollified, and waited patiently outside whilst the cunning old Queen prepared for his reception, which she did by cutting a hole in the very middle of a stool, putting a red-hot stone underneath, covering it over with a saucepan-lid, and then spreading a beautiful embroidered cloth over all.

Then she went to the door, and receiving the Rat with the greatest respect, led him to the stool, praying him to be seated.

"Dear! dear! how clever I am! What bargains I do make, to be sure!" said he to himself as he climbed on to the stool. "Here I am, son-in-law to a real live Queen! What will the neighbours say?"

At first he sat down on the edge of the stool, but even there it was warm, and after a while he began to fidget, saying, "Dear me, mother-in-law! how hot your house is! Everything I touch seems burning!"

"You are out of the wind there, my son," replied the cunning old Queen; "sit more in the middle of the stool, and then you will feel the breeze and get cooler."

But he didn't! for the saucepan-lid by this time had become so hot, that the Rat fairly frizzled when he sat down on it; and it was not until he had left all his tail, half his hair, and a large piece of his skin behind him, that be managed to escape, howling with pain, and vowing that never, never, never again would he make a bargain!

BABIOLE

"Babiole" tells the bizarre and endearing tale of a monkey raised into a princess at the French court. The title character is elegant and refined in every way but her physique, which does not hinder her as a very young creature moving among the human elite but does become a serious obstacle to her success in adult life. Rich with social commentary, this story was published in France in 1698 by the prolific writer Marie-Catherine le Jumel de Barneville, Comtesse d'Aulnoy (usually called "Madame d'Aulnoy"). For nearly two centuries d'Aulnoy's tales were enormously popular in English translations (the one that appears here dates to 1892), in adaptations for child readers, and as the basis for Christmas pantomimes. She is known today as the author who coined the term "conte de fées," which entered English as "fairy tale." Her stories can feel unexpectedly long and refreshingly complex to modern readers, but in their day they helped define what a fairy tale was: fantastical landscapes in which characters face social challenges, written as adult amusement and intellectual provocation. In this case, the character of Babiole seems to ask us, what is beauty worth? What does society do with people who embody social ideals on the inside but look different from the rest? These questions pose an ethical challenge, even today.

There was once a queen who had nothing left to wish for but to have children. She could talk of nothing else, and would constantly say that the Fairy Fanferluche, who had been present at her birth, and who bore a grudge

Marie-Catherine d'Aulnoy, "Babiole" (1698), translated by Miss Lee and Annie Macdonell, in *The Fairy Tales of Madame d'Aulnoy, Newly Done into English* (London: Lawrence and Bullen, 1892), 211–31.

against the queen, her mother, had flown into a rage, and had wished her nothing but ill-luck.

One day, as she sat alone grieving by the fireside, she saw a little old woman, no bigger than your hand, come down the chimney, riding on three reeds. On her head was a branch of hawthorn; her gown was of flies' wings, and two nutshells served for shoes. She rode through the air, sweeping three times round the room, and then stopped in front of the queen. "For a long time," she said, "you have been grumbling at me, saying I am to blame for your misfortunes, and that I am responsible for all that happens to you. You think, madam, that it is my fault you have no children. I come to announce to you the birth of an infanta, but I warn you she will cost you many a tear." "Ah! noble Fanferluche," exclaimed the queen, "do not deny me your pity and your aid; I undertake to do everything in my power for you if you will promise that the princess shall be a comfort to me and not a grief." "Fate is stronger than I," replied the fairy. "All that I can do to prove my affection for you is to give you this hawthorn. Fasten it to your daughter's head as soon as she is born; it will protect her from many perils." And, giving her the hawthorn, she vanished like a flash of lightning.

The queen remained sad and pondering. "What!" she said, "do I really desire a daughter who is to cost me many sighs and tears? Should I not be happier without her?" When the king, whom she dearly loved, was with her her troubles seemed more bearable. Her child would soon be born, and in preparation for the event she gave her attendants strict charge to fasten the hawthorn on the princess's head directly she should come into the world. She kept the branch in a golden box covered with diamonds, and valued it above all her possessions.

At length the queen gave birth to the loveliest creature that ever was seen. Without delay the hawthorn was fastened on her head, and at the same instant, wonderful to relate! she turned into a little monkey, and jumped and ran and capered about the room—a perfect monkey and no mistake! At this metamorphosis all the ladies uttered horrible cries, and the queen, more alarmed than any one, thought she should die of despair. She ordered the flowers to be taken off the creature's head. With the greatest difficulty the monkey was caught; but it was in vain that the fatal flowers were removed. She was already a monkey, a confirmed monkey. She could not suck nor do anything else like a child, and cared only about nuts and chestnuts.

"Wicked Fanferluche!" exclaimed the queen, sorrowfully, "what have I done that you should treat me so cruelly? What is to become of me? What a disgrace for me, that all my subjects should think I have brought a monster into the world! and how horrified the king will be at seeing such a child!" With tears she entreated her ladies to advise her what to do in this serious case. "Madam," said the oldest, "you must persuade the king that the princess is dead, and we must shut up this monkey in a box and cast it to the bottom of the sea; it would be a terrible thing to keep an animal of this sort any longer."

The queen had some scruple in making up her mind; but when she was told that the king was coming into her room, she became so confused and distressed that without further consideration she bid the lady-in-waiting do what she liked with the monkey.

It was carried into another apartment and shut up in a box. One of the queen's servants was ordered to throw it into the sea; and he at once set off with it. Now was the princess in the greatest danger; for the man, seeing that the box was beautiful, was very unwilling to throw it away. Sitting down by the sea-shore, he took the monkey out of the box, and, not knowing it was his sovereign, resolved to kill her. But while he held it in his hand a loud noise startled him and made him turn his head. He saw an open chariot drawn by six unicorns, glittering with gold and precious stones, and in front marched several trumpeters. A queen in royal robes and with a crown on her head was seated on cushions of cloth of gold, and held her four-year-old son on her knee.

The servant recognised the queen, for she was his mistress's sister and had come to rejoice with her. But as soon as she learned that the little princess was dead, she set out in great sadness to return to her own kingdom. She was startled from a deep reverie by her son crying out: "I want the monkey! I will have it"; and, on looking, the queen saw the prettiest monkey that ever was. The servant looked about for means of escape, but they would not let him go. The queen gave him a large sum of money; and, finding the monkey a gentle little plaything, called her Babiole, who thus, in spite of the cruelty of fate, fell into the hands of her aunt.

When she reached her own realms the little prince begged her to give him Babiole for a playmate. He wished her to be dressed like a princess; so every day new frocks were made for her. She was taught to walk only on her feet; and a prettier and nicer-looking monkey could nowhere be found. Her face was black as a jay's, and she wore a little white hood with bright red tufts at the ears. Her hands were no bigger than butterflies' wings, and the expression of her bright eyes was so intelligent that no one could be astonished at her accomplishments. When the prince, who was very fond of her, caressed her, as he was always doing, she took great care not to bite him; and when he cried she cried too.

She had been living four years with the queen when, one day, she began to stutter like a child trying to speak. Everyone was astonished, and still more so when she began to talk in a sweet and clear voice, and so distinctly that not a word was lost. Here was a marvel! Babiole talking! Babiole making herself understood by words! The queen sent for the monkey to amuse her; and, to the great disappointment of the prince, she was taken to the queen's apartment. It cost him some tears; and, to console him, dogs, cats, birds, and squirrels were given him, and even a pony, called Criquetin, who danced the saraband;* but all that did not make up for a word from Babiole. As for her, she was less at her ease with the queen than with the prince. She had to reply like a sybil to a hundred

* A slow dance in triple time.

witty and learned questions that she did not always understand. Directly an ambassador or a foreigner arrived she had to appear in a gown of velvet or brocade with stiff bodice and ruff. If the court was in mourning she wore a long mantle and crape, a costume that tired her very much. She was no longer permitted to eat what was to her taste: the doctor gave the orders, and these did not at all please her; for she was as self-willed as only a monkey born a princess could be.

The queen gave her masters who cultivated her bright wit. She excelled in playing on the harpsichord; and a wonderful instrument had been made for her out of an oyster-shell. Painters from the four quarters of the globe, and especially from Italy, came to paint her. Her fame flew from one end of the earth to the other, for never before had a talking monkey been heard of.

The prince, as beautiful as Cupid, and as full of grace and wit, was a prodigy no less extraordinary. He came to see Babiole, and sometimes played with her; and now and then their talk would turn from merry jests to serious subjects, and to moralising. Babiole had a heart; and it had not been metamorphosed like the rest of her little person; and she became so exceedingly fond of the prince that her affection began to be harmful to her. The unhappy Babiole did not know what to do. She passed her nights on the top of a window shutter, or in the chimney corner, and would not enter her clean, soft, downy, and padded basket. Her governess (for she had one) heard her often sigh, and sometimes she would utter her laments aloud. Her melancholy grew with her intelligence; and she never saw herself in a mirror without trying in her vexation to break it. For, as it used to be said, once an ape, always an ape, so Babiole could not get rid of the evil disposition natural to her race.

The prince had grown up. He liked hunting, dancing, the drama, feats of arms, and books, and rarely now gave the monkey a thought. With her it was quite otherwise. She loved him better at twelve than she had at six; but when she reproached him for his neglect he thought he made the amplest amends that could to be expected of him when he gave her a rosy apple or some candied chestnuts.

At last the fame of Babiole began to make a great sensation in Monkey-land, and Magot, the king of the monkeys, was greatly desirous of marrying her. For that purpose he sent a magnificent embassy to ask her hand from the queen. It was not difficult to explain his intentions to his chief ministers, but it would have been infinitely hard to express them to others without the aid of parrots and the birds commonly called magpies. They chattered a great deal; and the jays, who accompanied the procession, felt in honour bound to make as much noise as their companions.

A big ape, called Mirlifiche, was chief of the embassy. He had a coach made of pasteboard, on which were painted the loves of the King Magot with Monette, a monkey renowned throughout Monkeyland, who had died a cruel death by the claws of a wild cat that had taken her playfulness serious-ly. The delights that Magot and Monette had enjoyed during their married life, and the profound sorrow with which the king had wept for her after her death, were there depicted. Six white rabbits, of first-rate breed, drew the coach, called by distinction the state carriage. Behind came a chariot, in which were the monkeys destined to wait on Babiole. You should have seen how they were dressed! It really seemed as if they were going to a wedding. The rest of the procession was composed of little spaniels, young greyhounds, Spanish cats, Muscovy rats, a few hedgehogs, sly weasels, and greedy foxes. Some drove the chariots, others carried the baggage. Mirlifiche, graver than a Roman dictator, wiser than a Cato, rode a young hare, that ambled better than an English gelding.

The queen knew nothing of this magnificent embassy until it arrived at her palace. Hearing shouts of laughter from the people and the guards she put her head out of the window, and beheld the most extraordinary cavalcade she had ever seen in her life. Immediately Mirlifiche, followed by a considerable number of monkeys, approached the chariot of the ladies of his troop, and, giving his paw to the big one, called Gigona, he helped her to get down. Then letting loose the little parrot, who was to act as his interpreter, he waited while the beautiful bird was presented to the queen and begged an audience.

The parrot, mounting gently in the air, went to the window from which the queen was looking out, and said in the prettiest tone of voice imaginable: "Madam, his grace Count Mirlifiche, ambassador of the celebrated Magot, king of Monkeyland, begs an audience of your majesty, to discuss a very important question." "Pretty parrot," said the queen, caressing him, "first you must eat some roast meat and have something to drink. After that, you may go and tell Count Mirlifiche that he is heartily welcome to my realm, and so are all who accompany him. If he is not too much fatigued by his journey, he can presently enter the audience chamber, where I, on my throne, will await him with the whole court."

At these words the parrot kissed his claw twice, saluted the guard, sang a little tune to give vent to his joy, and taking to his wings again and perching on Mirlifiche's shoulder, whispered in his ear the favourable answer he had just received. Mirlifiche was fully sensible of the honour, and told the magpie Magot, who had been appointed as sub-interpreter, to ask one of the queen's officers to be good enough to give him a room in which to rest for a few moments. Accordingly, a saloon paved with coloured and gilded marble, one of the handsomest in the palace, was opened, and he entered with a part of his suite. But since monkeys are naturally very inquisitive, they smelt out a certain corner in which many pots of preserves had been stored. Immediately the gluttons set on it. One seized a crystal cup full of apricots, another a bottle of syrup; some took patties, others marzipan. The winged creatures who accompanied them were vexed at the sight of a repast where there was neither hemp nor millet seed; and a jay, by profession a great talker, flew into the audience chamber, and, respectfully approaching the queen, said: "Madam, I am too much your majesty's obedient servant to be a willing party to the havoc that is being made in your delicious preserves. Count Mirlifiche has already eaten three pots himself; he was gobbling up the fourth without the slightest respect for your royal majesty, when, deeply grieved, I came to warn you." "Many thanks, little jay, for your friendly thought," said the queen, smiling, "but you need not be so zealous for my pots of preserves; I relinquish them for the sake of Babiole, whom I love with all my heart." The jay, somewhat ashamed of the attack he had just made, withdrew without a word.

A few moments later the ambassador entered, accompanied by his suite. He was not dressed quite in the fashion, for since the famous Fagotin, who made such a brilliant figure in the world, had returned home, a good model had been lacking. He wore a sugar-loaf hat with a bunch of green feathers, a shoulder-belt of blue paper covered with gold spangles, deep frills to his breeches, and carried a cane. The parrot, who passed for something of a poet, having composed a very solemn harangue, advanced to the foot of the throne on which the queen was seated. Addressing Babiole, he spoke thus:—

"Learn the power of your eyes' bright fire
By the love that they in King Magot inspire!
These monkeys, birds, cats—all this splendid array
Are here, at his word, and his passion display.
Monette, the queen, beloved of her race—
Except you, none had ever so comely a face—
By a wild cat's claws she was mangled and torn,
And Magot, the king, was left all forlorn.
The king to her memory faithfulness swore,
And to love her forever and evermore;
But you, from his heart, by your sweet perfection,
Have chased of his first love all recollection.
In you now, madam, he finds all his delight;

And, could you but measure his passion's height,

No doubt but your heart, framed in pity's fashion

To cure his love, would share his passion.

For once on a time he was hearty and gay,

But now he is weak and thin always

As if pain bore him company every hour—

Ah! madam, indeed he feels love's power!

The olives and nuts that he found so good

Are now to his palate but tasteless food;

He dies!—'tis you alone that can save—

You alone can keep him on this side the grave.

On all the delights that your coming await

In our happy land, can I not dilate.

There figs and grapes will fail you never,

And the finest fruits are in season ever."

The parrot had no sooner finished his speech than the queen looked at Babiole, who was covered with confusion. Before replying, the queen, wishing to find out her feelings, asked the parrot to explain to the ambassador that, as far as she was concerned, she favoured his master's suit. The audience finished, she withdrew, and Babiole followed her into her closet. "My little one," she said, "I shall be very sorry to part with you, but it is not possible to refuse Magot, who asks your hand in marriage, for I have not yet forgotten that his father sent two hundred thousand monkeys into the field to carry on a great war against mine. They ate so many of our subjects that we were obliged to make an ignominious peace." "You mean, madam," answered Babiole, impatiently, "that, to avoid his wrath, you are resolved to sacrifice me to this wretched monster, but I at least implore your majesty to grant me a few days in which to make up my mind." "That is but fair," said the queen; "nevertheless, if you will take my advice, decide quickly. Consider the honours in store for you, the magnificence of the embassy, and the number of ladies-in-waiting sent to you. I am sure that Magot never did for Monette what he has done for you." "I do not know what he did for Monette," replied little Babiole, disdainfully, "but I do know that I care very little for these marks of affection for me." Then she rose, and, gracefully curtseying, sought the prince to tell him her troubles. As soon as he saw her, he cried out: "Well, my Babiole, when are we to dance at your wedding?" "I do not know, sir," she said, sadly; "but I am so wretched that I have no longer the strength to keep my secret from you; and, although it ill becomes my modesty, I must confess to you that you are the only one I wish for a husband." "Husband!" said the prince, bursting out laughing, "husband, little one! Well, that is delightful! but all the same, I trust, you will excuse me if I do not accept your proposal, for, to tell the truth, in our persons, our appearance, and our manners, we are not exactly a match." "I agree with you," she said, "especially since our hearts are not alike. For a long while I have seen that you are ungrateful, and I am extremely foolish to love a prince who so little deserves it." "But, Babiole," said he, "think of the trouble I should be in to see you perched on the top of a sycamore, holding on to a branch by the end of your tail. Come now, let this be a joke, and for your honour and mine marry the monkey king, and, in token of our firm friendship, send me your first little Magot." "It is fortunate for you, sir, that my nature is not entirely that of a monkey. Any other than myself would have already torn out your eyes, bitten off your nose, and wrenched off your ears; but I leave you to the reflections your unworthy conduct will one day cause you." She could say no more. Her governess came to fetch her, the ambassador Mirlifiche having entered her apartment with magnificent presents.

There was a costume made of a spider's web, embroidered with tiny glow worms, an egg-shell case for combs. A white-heart cherry served for a pin cushion, and all the linen was trimmed with paper lace. In a basket there were several carefully-chosen shells, some to serve for earrings, others for bodkins, all of them shining like diamonds; and, what was even better, a dozen boxes full of sweetmeats, and a little glass chest with a hazel-nut and an olive inside. But the key of this was lost, and Babiole troubled little about it.

The ambassador gave her to understand, in the chattering language of Monkeyland, that his sovereign was more touched by her charms than he had ever been by those of any other monkey; that he intended to build her a palace at the top of a fir tree; that he sent these gifts and the fine preserves as a mark of his attachment; and that indeed the king, his master, could prove his affection in no better way. "But," he added, "the strongest testimony to his love, and that which you ought to feel most deeply, is, madam, the trouble he has been at to have his picture painted, so that you may anticipate the pleasure of seeing him." He then displayed the portrait of the King of the Monkeys, seated on a huge log, eating an apple.

Babiole turned away her head that she might not look longer on so ugly a face, and after some little display of temper gave Mirlifiche to understand that she thanked his master for his esteem, but that, as yet, she had not made up her mind whether she intended to marry at all.

Meanwhile, the queen determined not to draw down on herself the anger of the monkeys, and, believing there would be little difficulty in sending Babiole wherever she wished her to go, had everything prepared for her departure. At this news, despair took possession of Babiole. The prince's disdain on one hand, the queen's indifference on the other, and more than all that, the prospect of such a husband, made her resolve to run away. It was not a very difficult matter, for, since she could speak, she was no longer tied up, and came and went as she liked, and would enter her room as often by the window as by the door.

She set out as quickly as possible, jumping from tree to tree, from branch to branch, until she came to the bank of a river. The violence of her despair blinded her to the danger she was running into in attempting to cross by swimming. Without the least consideration she threw herself in, and immediately went to the bottom. But there she did not lose consciousness; she saw a magnificent grotto, adorned with shells. She hastened in, and was received by a venerable old man, whose white beard reached to his waist. He was lying on a bed of reeds and irises, with a crown of poppies and wild lilies on his head, and propped up against a rock, from whence flowed several springs that fed the river.

"Well! what brings you here, my little Babiole?" said he, reaching her his hand. "Sir," she replied, "I am an unfortunate monkey; I am running away from a hideous ape, to whom they wish to marry me." "I know more about you than you think," added the wise old man. "It is true you detest Magot, but it is equally true that you love a young prince who cares nothing for you." "Ah! sir," cried Babiole, sighing, "do not let us speak of him. The recollection of him only makes my sorrows harder to bear." "He will not be always insensible to love," continued the King of the Fish; "I know he is reserved for the most beautiful princess in the world." "Unhappy wretch that I am!" continued Babiole; "then he will never be mine!" The old man smiled, and said: "Do not grieve, my good Babiole. Time is a wonderful master. Only take care not to lose the little glass chest Magot sent you, and that you have, perchance, now in your pocket. I can tell you no more. Here is a tortoise that travels at a good rate. Seat yourself on her; she will take you where you have to go." "After what I owe you," said Babiole, "I cannot help wishing to know your name." "I am called," he said, "Biroquoi, father of Biroquie, a river, as you see, of considerable size and fame."

Babiole mounted her tortoise with the greatest confidence. For a long time they floated over the water, and at length, by what seemed a very roundabout way, the tortoise gained the bank. It would be difficult to imagine anything prettier than the side saddle and the rest of the trappings. There were even little horse-pistols, for which two crab-shells served as cases.

Babiole was journeying on with the utmost confidence in wise Biroquoi's promises when she suddenly heard a great noise. Alas! alas! it was the ambassador Mirlifiche, with all his attendants, returning to Monkey-land, sad and sorrowful at Babiole's flight. A monkey belonging to the troop had, during the halt for dinner, climbed a nut tree, in order to throw down nuts to feed the little ones; but no sooner had he reached the top of the tree than, looking round on every side, he saw Babiole on the poor tortoise, who was slowly making her way across the open country. At sight of her he began to shout so loudly that the assembled monkeys asked him, in their language, what was the matter. He told them, and immediately the magpies and jays were let loose, and they flew to where she was. On their report, the ambassador, the monkeys, and the rest of the company ran and stopped her.

Here was a misfortune for Babiole! Nothing more unlucky or disagree-able could possibly have happened. She was forced to get into the state car-riage, which was immediately surrounded by the most vigilant monkeys, by a few foxes, and a cock who, perched on the top, kept guard day and night. A monkey led the tortoise along as a rare animal, and so the cavalcade con-tinued its journey, to the great sorrow of Babiole, whose sole companion was Madam Gigona, a cross-grained and disagreeable monkey.

At the end of three days, which passed without adventure, the guides having lost their way, they reached a large and magnificent city, whose name they did not know; but, seeing a beautiful garden with the gate standing open, they stopped there, and plundered it, as if it had been a conquered country. One crunched nuts, another gobbled cherries, a third despoiled a plum tree. Indeed, there was not the smallest monkey but joined in the pillage, and laid in a store.

You must know that this city was the capital of the kingdom where Babiole was born; her mother lived there, and since she had had the mis-fortune to see her daughter changed into a monkey by means of a haw-thorn branch, had never allowed a monkey, a baboon, or an ape to remain in the kingdom, nor, indeed, anything that could recall to her mind the deplorable and fatal circumstance. A monkey was looked upon as a disturber of the public peace. Think, then, what was the astonishment of the people to see a pasteboard coach, a chariot of painted straw, and all the rest of the most extraordinary cavalcade that was ever seen since tales were tales, and fairies fairies!

The news spread quickly to the palace. The queen was paralysed; she thought the whole race of monkeys meant to make an attack on her government. She immediately summoned her council, who, by her orders, found the whole troop guilty of high treason, and, not wishing to lose the opportunity of making such an example of them as should be remembered in the future, she sent her officers into the garden with orders to seize them all. Big nets were cast over the trees, and the capture was soon effected. In spite of the respect due to the rank of an ambassador, this high office was most contemptuously treated in the person of Mirlifiche, who was pitilessly cast into the depths of a cellar under a big empty cask, where he and his companions were imprisoned, with the lady monkeys, both matrons and damsels, who accompanied Babiole.

As for Babiole, she felt a secret joy at this fresh disturbance. When misfortunes reach a certain point nothing further is dreaded, and death itself seems desirable. Such was her condition, for her heart was full of the prince who disdained her, and her mind occupied with the horrible thought of King Magot, whose wife she was on the point of becoming.

Besides, we must not forget to mention that she was so prettily dressed, and her manners were so distinguished, that those who had seized her, stopped to look at her as something quite marvellous, and when she spoke to them they were still more surprised, for they had already heard of the wonderful Babiole. The queen who had found her, and who did not know of her niece's metamorphosis, had often written to her sister that she possessed an extraordinary monkey, and begged her to come and see it, but the unhappy queen would pass over that sentence without reading it.

At length the warders, carried away by admiration, brought Babiole into a big gallery and made her a little throne. She sat on it more like a sovereign than a captive monkey, and the queen, happening to pass by, was so vastly taken with her pretty face and the charming compliments she paid her, that, in spite of herself, the nature within her made appeal for the infanta. She took her in her arms; and, as for the little creature, feelings she had never known before stirred within her. She threw herself on the queen's neck and spoke such loving and engaging words that all who heard her were delighted. "No, madam," she exclaimed, "it is not the fear of approaching death, with which I am told you threaten the unfortunate race of monkeys, that terrifies me and makes me try to please you and soften your heart. The cutting short of my life is by no means the greatest misfortune that can happen to me, and I have in me feelings so far above my condition that I should regret any step whatsoever that might be taken to preserve my life. It is you yourself I love. Your crown is of far less consequence to me than your goodness."

I ask you, what reply could be made when Babiole spoke such winning words? The queen said not a word, but opened her two eyes wide, seemed to consider, and felt her heart strangely stirred.

She carried the monkey into her closet, and when they were alone she said to her: "Tell me your adventures without a moment's delay, for I feel that of all the animals who inhabit the menageries, and whom I keep in my palace, you will be the one I shall love most. I assure you that for your sake I will pardon the monkeys who accompany you." "Ah! madam," she exclaimed, "I ask nothing for them. By ill-luck I was born a monkey, and that same ill-luck gave me intelligence that will cause me suffering till I die. For what must I feel when I see myself in my mirror: little, ugly, and sooty, my hands covered with hair, with a tail, and with teeth ever ready to bite; while, at the same time, I do not lack intelligence, and have taste, refinement, and quick feelings?" "Do you know what it is to love?" said the queen. Babiole sighed, but did not answer. "Oh!" continued the queen, "you must tell me if you love a monkey, a rabbit, or a squirrel; for, if you are not already too deeply pledged, I have a dwarf who will just suit you." At that proposal Babiole looked so disdainful that the queen burst out laughing. "Don't be angry," she said, "and tell me how it is that you can speak."

"All that I know of my adventures," replied Babiole, "is that your sister had scarcely left you after the birth and death of your daughter, when going along the sea-shore she saw one of your servants on the point of drowning me. At her command I was taken from him. By a miracle, that equally astonished everybody, speech and reason were given to me. Masters, who taught me several languages and to play musical instruments, were provided for me. At length, madam, I became aware of my misfortune, and—but," she exclaimed, seeing the queen's face pale and covered with a cold perspiration, "what is the matter, madam? I observe an extraordinary change in your appearance." "I am dying!" said the queen, in a weak, almost inaudible voice, "I am dying; my beloved and only too unhappy daughter! have I at last found you again!" At these words she swooned. Babiole, terrified, ran and called for aid. The queen's ladies hurried to give her water, to unlace her and put her to bed. Babiole crept in with her, and she was so small that no one noticed her.

When the queen had recovered from the long swoon into which the princess's words had thrown her, she desired to be left alone with the ladies who knew the fatal secret of her daughter's birth. She told them what had happened, and they were so dismayed that they did not know what advice to give.

But the queen commanded them to tell her what they considered it expedient to do in this lamentable case. Some said the monkey must be strangled, others that she should be shut up in a den; others, even, that she should be again thrown into the sea. The queen wept and sobbed. "She has so much intelligence," said she; "what a pity to see her reduced to this miserable condition by an enchanted bouquet! But, after all," continued she, "she is my daughter; it is I who brought on her the wicked Fanferluche's anger. Is it right that she should suffer on account of that fairy's hatred for me?" "Yes, madam," exclaimed her old lady-in-waiting, "your reputation must be saved. What would the world think if you declared that a little monkey was your daughter? It's not in nature to have such children when one is as beautiful as you." The queen lost patience at hearing her talk thus. But the old lady and the others were equally persistent that the little monster must be got rid of; and, finally, she determined to shut Babiole up in a castle, where she would be well fed and kindly treated, for the rest of her life.

When Babiole heard that the queen intended to put her in prison, she slipped quietly out by the side of the bed, and, throwing herself from the window on to a tree in the garden, escaped to the big forest, and left everybody in confusion at her loss. She spent the night in the hollow of an oak, where she had leisure to reflect on the cruelty of her fate. What caused her most distress was to be forced to leave the queen; but she preferred voluntary exile and the preservation of her liberty to the loss of it forever.

As soon as it was light she continued her journey, without knowing where she wished to go, thinking and thinking a thousand times over of the strangeness of this most extraordinary adventure. "What a difference," she exclaimed, "between what I am and what I was meant to be!" Tears flowed freely from poor Babiole's little eyes.

Directly day appeared she set out, fearing the queen would send after her, or that one of the monkeys escaped from the cellar would take her, against her will, to King Magot. She went on by slow degrees without following road or path until she reached a great desert, where there was neither house, nor tree, nor fruit, nor grass, nor spring. She entered it without thinking; and, only when she began to feel hungry, recognised too late that travelling in such a country was exceedingly imprudent.

Two days and two nights went by without her being able to catch even a grub or a fly. The fear of death seized on her, and she was so weak that she was on the point of swooning. She sank down on the ground; and, remembering the olive and the hazel nut in the little glass box, she thought they might make her a slight repast. Delighted at this ray of hope, she took a stone, broke the box to pieces, and crunched the olive.

But she had scarcely put her teeth in it when a great quantity of scented oil came pouring out upon her paws, which immediately turned into the most beautiful hands in the world. Her surprise was extreme: she took the oil and rubbed herself all over. Oh! wondrous! she immediately became so beautiful that there was nothing in the world like her. She felt that she had big eyes, a small mouth and a well-shaped nose. She was dying for a mirror; and at length managed to improvise one out of the biggest piece of the glass box. And when she saw herself, what joy! What a delightful surprise! Her clothes grew in size like herself; her head was well dressed; her hair fell in thousands of curls; her complexion was fresh as the flowers in spring. The first moments of surprise over, hunger made itself more acutely felt, and her distress vastly increased. "What!" she said, "so young and so beautiful, a born princess, and I must perish in this barren place! Oh! wretched fate that led me here! How strangely is my destiny shaped! Have you made so delightful and unexpected a change in me only to make my troubles greater? And you, venerable river Biroquie, who so generously saved my life, will you leave me to perish in this frightful solitude?"

In vain did the infanta implore help—the whole world was deaf to her voice. Hunger tormented her to such a degree that she took the hazel nut and cracked it; but, in throwing away the shell, she was greatly surprised to see come out of it architects, painters, masons, upholsterers, sculptors, and ever so many other sorts of workmen. Some made designs for a palace, others built it; others, again, furnished it. Some decorated the rooms, and some cultivated the gardens; everything shone with gold and azure. A magnificent banquet was served; sixty princesses, more beautifully dressed than queens, accompanied by squires and followed by pages, came to her with charming compliments, and invited her to the feast that awaited her. Babiole at once, without waiting to be entreated, advanced quickly, with the air of a queen, into the hall, where she ate ravenously of the food.

Scarcely had she left the table when her treasurers brought her fifteen thousand chests, big as hogsheads, filled with gold and diamonds. They asked her if she was agreeable that they should pay the workmen who had built her palace. She replied that was only right, on condition that they would also build a city, marry, and remain with her. They all consented; and, although the city was five times bigger than Rome, it was finished in three quarters of an hour. Surely these were wonders enough to come out of a little hazel nut!

The princess was considering in her mind whether she should send an imposing embassy to her mother, and some reproachful messages to her cousin, the young prince. While the necessary measures were being taken she amused herself with looking on at the tilting, where she always awarded the prize, with cards, the play, hunting and fishing, for a river had been brought into her domain. The fame of her beauty spread over the whole world: kings from the four corners of the earth came to her court with giants taller than mountains, and pigmies smaller than rats.

It happened that on a certain day a great tournament was being held. Several knights entered the lists. They got angry with each other, came to blows, and were wounded. The princess, in great wrath, came down from the balcony to see who were the guilty men: but when they were disarmed, what was her distress to see the prince, her cousin! If he was not dead, he was very nearly so, and she thought she must herself die of surprise and grief. She had him carried into the finest apartment of the palace, where nothing necessary for his cure was wanting—physicians from Chodrai, surgeons, salves, broths, and syrups. The infanta herself made the bandages and prepared the lint. Her eyes moistened them with tears, and such tears must have been balm to the sick man. For, indeed, he was ill in more ways than one; not to reckon a

NANINA'S SHEEP

Sheep roam through the pastures of many stories, from parable to nursery rhyme to literature—Jesus and Little Bo Peep watch over them, wolves wear their fur to pass unnoticed, Alice finds one tending shop in her travels through the looking glass, and we even count them to calm our minds before sleep. They give a landscape an idyllic charm, one that was popular with the Victorian contemporaries of writer Mary de Morgan. De Morgan wrote three successful volumes of fairy tales and played creatively (sometimes subversively) with conventional expectations of the genre. In this sense, De Morgan's fairy tale follows in a long tradition of tale writing and telling, drawing on deeply familiar cultural stereotypes and then asking her audience to see them in a fresh way. Nanina's adventure gives sheep an idyllic role, but their presence does not have the effect that one might expect. Instead of calming her spirits, the pastoral landscape roars to life with a herd of black goats and their beautiful goatherd (called a "shepherd" in this tale), whose music making and merriment seem irresistible. In fact, the world turns upside down: what looks like an enchanted dream turns out to be a nightmare. The shepherdess and her sheep lose each other to a hypnotic musical ritual they cannot control and find each other again thanks to Nanina's resolve, suffering, and a kindly, if rough, force of nature: a beech tree. Associated in European folk traditions with knowledge, thresholds, and rites of birth and death, the beech tree is both richly symbolic and an important character in this story. How do people and animals and nature coexist? Can apparent benevolence be cruel and apparent cruelty be benevolent? De Morgan sends us into the fields and pastures to think about it.

Mary de Morgan, "Nanina's Sheep," in *The Windfairies and Other Tales* (London: Seeley, 1900), 65–80.

Once there lived a young girl called Nanina, who kept sheep for an old farmer. One day he said to her, "Nanina, I'm going away to buy pigs at a market far off, and I shall be away one whole month, so be sure and take good care of the flock, and remember, there are six sheep and eight lambs, and I must find them safe when I return. And mind, Nanina, that whatever you do, you don't go near the old palace on the other side of the hill, for it is filled with wicked fairies who might do you an ill turn." Nanina promised, and her master started.

The first day all went well, and she drove the flock in safely at night; but the next day she found it dull sitting on the hillside watching the lambs at play, and wondered why her master had told her always to keep on that side, and away from the old palace on the other.

"If it is filled with fairies," quoth she, "it won't hurt me just to look at it; I should like to see a fairy." So she drove her flock to the other side of the hill, and sat looking at the old palace that was half in ruins, but was said to be lit up quite brightly every night after it was dark.

"I wonder if it really is lit up," said Nanina, "I should like to see." So she waited on that side of the hill till the sun went down, and then she saw a bright light appearing in one of the palace windows. As she stood and watched, the front door opened, and out there came a shepherd boy followed by a flock of black goats. Nanina stared at him, for she had never seen anyone so beautiful before. He was dressed in glittering green, and wore a soft brown hat trimmed with leaves under which his curls hung down. In one hand he held a crook and in the other a pipe, and as he drew near, he began to play the pipe and dance merrily, while the goats behind him skipped and danced too. Nanina had never seen such goats; they were jet black, with locks curling and thick and soft as silk. As she listened open-mouthed to the music of the pipe, she heard it speak words in its playing—

"When the young birds sing,
And the young plants spring,

Then dance we so merrily together, oh."

The shepherd boy danced lightly to where she stood, and louder and louder sounded the pipe, and still it said—

"When the young birds sing,
And the young plants spring,
Then dance we so merrily together, oh."

Nanina gaped to see the goats dance and spring in time to the music, and so cheering it was, that she felt her own feet beginning to move with it. The shepherd made her a low bow and offered her his hand, and she placed hers in it, and off they started together. Nanina's feet felt as light as if they had been made of cork, and she laughed with glee as she bounded on; and as she danced with the shepherd, so her flock began to move too, and thus they went, followed by the black goats and sheep all skipping merrily. "If my flock follow me there can be no harm," thought Nanina, and on they kept in time to the wonderful tune—

"When the young birds sing,
And the young plants spring,
Then dance we so merrily together, oh."

Whither they went she knew not, she thought of nothing but the joy of dancing to the wonderful music; but suddenly, just ere sunrise, the shepherd stopped, and dropped her hand and gave one long slow note on the pipe, at which the goats gathered round him, and before she knew where they were going, they had disappeared into the palace. Then she was in a terrible fright, for she saw the sun beginning to rise, and found the whole night had passed, when she thought she had only been ten minutes. She counted her sheep, and, alas! there was one lamb missing. She sought everywhere for it, but no trace of it was to be seen. Then she drove all the others back to the farm and

COSTANTINO FORTUNATO

This sixteenth-century Italian story of a clever and resourceful cat improving the fortunes of its human master is best known through a related French story published over a century later by Charles Perrault—what English readers know as "Puss in Boots." This earlier fairy tale by the Venetian writer Giovan Francesco Straparola foregrounds its humble human hero in its title, "Costantino Fortunato," but there's no question that the cat is the most interesting and important character in the story. Male trickster figures abound in oral traditions, but they are often figured as driven by bodily desires, unfettered by social conventions, culturally central but socially marginalized. Straparola's cat, on the other hand, is female and might be seen as a maverick in her day. She pairs recognizably feline traits (moving quickly from hunting to grooming) with significant accomplishments in the human world: securing office with the king, masterminding Costantino's rise to wealth, and slyly acquiring land. Her remarkable skill with a ruse puts her in the company of other enchanted creatures, such as sorcerers and fairies, rather than conventional heroines or even heroes. And this cat uses her mouth for more than the slaughter of prey and tender care of her master's body: she works magic with her words, knowing just what to say to get what she desires. What kind of power is this? Straparola's Piacevoli notti *(Pleasant Nights), from which this tale comes, draws on local Italian folklore, fable, literature, and science to produce bawdy characters that were surprising in their day. What he could probably not imagine is that Costantino's cat would still look pretty radical in twenty-first-century North America. What literary company would she keep today?*

Giovan Francesco Straparola, "Costantino Fortunato" (1553), translated by Nancy Canepa, 2011, in *Marvelous Transformations: An Anthology of Fairy Tales and Contemporary Critical Perspectives*, edited by Christine A. Jones and Jennifer Schacker (Peterborough, Ontario: Broadview, 2013), 106–8.

So often, my lovely ladies, you see the richest of men fall into great poverty, but also the most destitute rise to a high state. This is what happened to one poor little fellow, who started out as a beggar, and then attained royal status.

In Bohemia there once was a woman by the name of Soriana, who was extremely poor and had three sons, the first of whom was called Dusolino, the second Tesifone, and the third Costantino Fortunato. She had nothing of substance in the world but three things: a kneading chest that women use to prepare bread, a peel on which they bake bread, and a cat. Soriana was already heavy with years, and as she neared death, she made up her last will and testament. To Dusolino, her oldest son, she left the kneading chest; to Tesifone the peel; and to Costantino the cat.

When the mother had died and been buried, the neighboring women began asking to borrow the chest and the peel for their own needs, and since they knew that the boys were extremely poor, they would make them pizza, which Dusolino and Tesifone ate without sharing any part of it with their younger brother Costantino. And if Costantino asked them for something, they answered that he should go ask his cat to give it to him. And so poor Costantino, together with his cat, suffered greatly. But the cat, who was enchanted, felt compassion for Costantino and, angry with the two brothers who treated him so cruelly, said, "Costantino, don't be sad, for I intend to provide for both your and my own lives."

The cat left the house and went out to the country, where, pretending to be asleep, she caught a passing hare and killed it. Then she went to the royal palace, and when she saw some courtiers she told them that she wanted to speak with the king. The king, hearing that it was a cat who wanted to speak to him, had her summoned and asked her what sort of request she brought. The cat answered that her master, Costantino, was sending him a gift of a hare that he had caught, and she presented it to the king. The king accepted the gift, and asked the cat who this Costantino was. The cat answered that he was a man whose goodness, beauty, and power had no superiors. At this, the king gave the cat the warmest of receptions, offering her delectable things to eat and to drink. When the cat was well sated, with a sleight of paw and without being seen by anyone she filled her knapsack, which was next to her, with some of the fine victuals. Then she asked the king's permission to leave, and brought the food to Costantino.

When his brothers saw the food that Costantino was enjoying, they asked him to share it with them, but he returned their favor and refused. And this gave rise to a burning envy, which continuously gnawed at their hearts.

Although Costantino had a handsome face, on account of all his suffering he was infected with scabies and ringworm, which were of great annoyance to him. But then he went with his cat to the river and was diligently licked and smoothed, and in a few days he was completely free of disease.

The cat continued, as we have described, to present gifts at the royal palace, and in this way supported her master. But at a certain point the cat grew tired of going back and forth, and was afraid that she might be considered a nuisance by the king's courtiers, and she said to her master, "Sir, if you do what I order you to, I will make you rich in a short time." "And how will you do that?" asked her master. The cat replied, "Come with me; your search has ended, for I'm more than willing to turn you into a rich man."

And so they went together to a spot by the river that was close to the royal palace. The cat undressed her master and, by common consent, threw him in the river, after which she began to shout loudly, "Help, help, come quickly, come quickly, mister Costantino is drowning!"

When the king heard this, he considered how many times he had received gifts from this fellow, and sent his people to help. Mister Costantino got out of the water and was dressed in fine clothes, and then was brought before the king, who received him with great ceremony. When the king asked Costantino why he had been thrown into the river, his painful condition did not allow him to answer, but the cat, who was always there right next to him, said, "You must know, O king, that some thieves had been informed that my master was carrying a load of jewels that he planned to give to you. They stripped him of everything he had and, intending to put him to death, they threw him in the river. Only by the mercy of these gentlemen was he saved from death."

Upon hearing this, the king ordered that Costantino be cleaned and well taken care of. And since he saw that he was handsome and knew that he was rich, he determined to give him his daughter Elisetta for a wife, providing her with a dowry of gold and precious gems, as well as splendid garments.

When the marriage had been celebrated and the triumphal processions had ended, the king ordered ten mules to be loaded with gold, and five others with the most ornate of garments, and he sent his daughter off to her husband's home, accompanied by many of his own men. Costantino saw how respectable and rich he had become, and did not know where to take his wife. He conferred with his cat, who said, "No need to worry, master, we'll take care of everything."

As everyone was happily riding along, the cat hurried quickly ahead, and when she was at quite a distance from the rest of the group, she came across some knights, to whom she said, "What are you doing here, you poor men? Take your leave at once, for a great cavalcade is about to arrive, and they're planning to attack you; here they are, they're getting closer, you can hear the clamor of their whinnying horses."

The frightened knights said, "What shall we do, then?" To which the cat replied, "This is what you are to do. If you're asked whose knights you are, you must answer bravely, 'Mister Costantino's,' and you will not be bothered."

When the cat had advanced farther down the road, she came across an enormous herd of sheep and oxen, and did something similar with their owners. And to whomever else she encountered she told the same thing.

The people accompanying Elisetta asked, "Whose knights are you, and whose fine herds are these?" And everyone answered in unison, "Mister Costantino's." Those accompanying the bride said, "So, then, mister Costantino, are we beginning to enter into your holdings?" And he nodded his head yes.

And he answered yes in the same way to everything that was asked of him, so that the company judged him to be an immensely wealthy man.

The cat arrived at a magnificent castle, where she found a small party of people, and said, "What are you doing, honorable men? Aren't you aware of your impending ruin?" "What are you talking about?" said the residents of the castle. "In less than an hour a band of soldiers will arrive here, and they will cut you to pieces. Don't you hear the horses whinnying? Don't you see the dust in the air? If you don't want to perish, take my advice, and you will all be safe. If anyone asks you whose castle this is, you must say, 'it belongs to mister Costantino Fortunato.'" And so they did.

When the noble company had reached the lovely castle, they asked the caretakers whom it belonged to and they replied, in spirited fashion, "To mister Costantino Fortunato." And so they entered the castle, and were honorably lodged.

The lord of that castle was sir Valentino, a valorous soldier, who a short time earlier had left the castle to bring his newly wedded wife home. But to his misfortune, before he arrived at the place where his beloved wife was waiting for him, he had a sudden and terrible accident on account of which he immediately died. And so Costantino Fortunato was left to be lord of the castle.

Not much time had elapsed before Morando, king of Bohemia, died. The people proclaimed their desire to have Costantino Fortunato become their king, since as the husband of Elisetta, daughter of the dead king, the succession to the throne was due him. And in this way Costantino went from being a pauper and a beggar to a lord and a king, and lived a long time with his Elisetta, and left many heirs to the throne.

EAST O' THE SUN, WEST O' THE MOON

Immensely powerful and elusive, polar bears sometimes take starring roles in the folk-lore and tale traditions of the northern peoples who share their habitat. The Norwegian tale known in English as "East o' the Sun, West o' the Moon" was collected from oral tradition by the folklorists Peter Christen Asbjørnsen and Jørgen Engebretsen Moe and became popular in Victorian England when translated in 1859. This magical tale features a white bear able to offer great wealth to a poor family—in exchange for a human bride. As in the classical story "Cupid and Psyche," the young woman in "East o' the Sun, West o' the Moon" is overcome by curiosity about the human form her bear takes in the darkness of night. Enchanted by the beauty of his sleeping form, she falls in love with this man—but in sneaking a look at him, she also plays a part in the unfolding of a spell cast by his troll stepmother. In some ways this story resonates with the better-known "Beauty and the Beast" and certainly blurs the lines between beauty and beastliness. Notably, "East o' the Sun, West o' the Moon" casts its heroine in an actively heroic role: only she can save her beloved, and to do so she must mobilize a combination of courage,

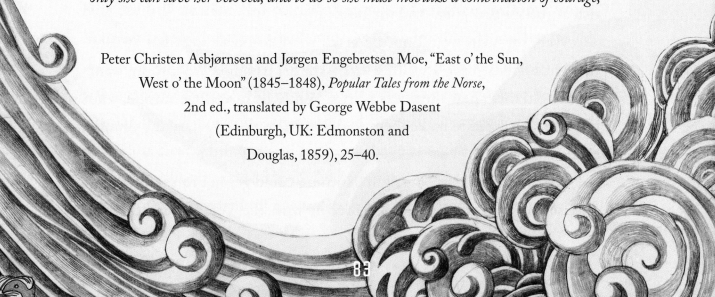

Peter Christen Asbjørnsen and Jørgen Engebretsen Moe, "East o' the Sun,
West o' the Moon" (1845–1848), *Popular Tales from the Norse*,
2nd ed., translated by George Webbe Dasent
(Edinburgh, UK: Edmonston and
Douglas, 1859), 25–40.

but at last she began to get silent and sorrowful; for there she went about all day alone, and she longed to go home to see her father and mother, and brothers and sisters. So one day, when the White Bear asked what it was that she lacked, she said it was so dull and lonely there, and how she longed to go home to see her father and mother, and brothers and sisters, and that was why she was so sad and sorrowful, because she couldn't get to them.

"Well, well!" said the Bear, "perhaps there's a cure for all this; but you must promise me one thing, not to talk alone with your mother, but only when the rest are by to hear; for she'll take you by the hand and try to lead you into a room alone to talk; but you must mind and not do that, else you'll bring bad luck on both of us."

So one Sunday the White Bear came and said now they could set off to see her father and mother. Well, off they started, she sitting on his back; and they went far and long. At last they came to a grand house, and there her brothers and sisters were running about out of doors at play, and everything was so pretty, 'twas a joy to see.

"This is where your father and mother live now," said the White Bear; "but don't forget what I told you, else you'll make us both unlucky."

"No! bless her, she'd not forget"; and when she had reached the house, the White Bear turned right about and left her.

Then when she went in to see her father and mother, there was such joy, there was no end to it. None of them thought they could thank her enough for all she had done for them. Now, they had everything they wished, as good as good could be, and they all wanted to know how she got on where she lived.

Well, she said, it was very good to live where she did; she had all she wished. What she said beside I don't know; but I don't think any of them had the right end of the stick, or that they got much out of her. But so in the afternoon, after they had done dinner, all happened as the White Bear had said.

Her mother wanted to talk with her alone in her bed-room; but she minded what the White Bear had said, and wouldn't go up stairs.

"Oh! what we have to talk about, will keep," she said, and put her mother off. But somehow or other, her mother got round her at last, and she had to tell her the whole story. So she said, how every night, when she had gone to bed, a man came and lay down beside her as soon as she had put out the light, and how she never saw him, because he was always up and away before the morning dawned; and how she went about woeful and sorrowing, for she thought she should so like to see him, and how all day long she walked about there alone, and how dull, and dreary, and lonesome it was.

"My!" said her mother; "it may well be a Troll you slept with! But now I'll teach you a lesson how to set eyes on him. I'll give you a bit of candle, which you can carry home in your bosom; just light that while he is asleep, but take care not to drop the tallow on him."

Yes! she took the candle, and hid it in her bosom, and as night drew on, the White Bear came and fetched her away.

But when they had gone a bit of the way, the White Bear asked if all hadn't happened as he had said?

"Well, she couldn't say it hadn't."

"Now, mind," said he, "if you have listened to your mother's advice, you have brought bad luck on us both, and then, all that has passed between us will be as nothing."

"No," she said, "she hadn't listened to her mother's advice."

So when she reached home, and had gone to bed, it was the old story over again. There came a man and lay down beside her; but at dead of night, when she heard he slept, she got up and struck a light, lit the candle, and let the light shine on him, and so she saw that he was the loveliest Prince one ever set eyes on, and she fell so deep in love with him on the spot, that she thought she couldn't live if she didn't give him a kiss there and then. And so she did, but as she kissed him, she dropped three hot drops of tallow on his shirt, and he woke up.

"What have you done?" he cried; "now you have made us both unlucky, for had you held out only this one year, I had been freed. For I have a stepmother who has bewitched me, so that I am a White Bear by day, and a Man by night. But now all ties are snapt between us; now I must set off from you to her. She lives in a Castle which stands EAST O' THE SUN AND WEST O' THE MOON, and there, too, is a Princess, with a nose three ells long, and she's the wife I must have now."

She wept and took it ill, but there was no help for it; go he must.

Then she asked if she mightn't go with him?

No, she mightn't.

"Tell me the way, then," she said, "and I'll search you out; *that* surely I may get leave to do."

"Yes, she might do that," he said; "but there was no way to that place. It lay EAST O' THE SUN AND WEST O' THE MOON, and thither she'd never find her way."

So next morning, when she woke up, both Prince and castle were gone, and then she lay on a little green patch, in the midst of the gloomy thick wood, and by her side lay the same bundle of rags she had brought with her from her old home.

So when she had rubbed the sleep out of her eyes, and wept till she was tired, she set out on her way, and walked many, many days, till she came to a lofty crag. Under it sat an old hag, and played with a gold apple which she tossed about. Her the lassie asked if she knew the way to the Prince, who lived with his stepmother in the Castle, that lay EAST O' THE SUN AND WEST O' THE MOON, and who was to marry the Princess with a nose three ells long.

"How did you come to know about him?" asked the old hag; "but maybe you are the lassie who ought to have had him?"

Yes, she was.

"So, so; it's you, is it?" said the old hag. "Well, all I know about him is, that he lives in the castle that lies EAST O' THE SUN AND WEST O' THE MOON, and thither you'll come, late or never; but still you may have the loan of my horse, and on him you can ride to my next neighbour. Maybe she'll be able to tell you; and when you get there, just give the horse a switch under the left ear, and beg him to be off home; and, stay, this gold apple you may take with you."

So she got upon the horse, and rode a long long time, till she came to another crag, under which sat another old hag, with a gold carding-comb. Her the lassie asked if she knew the way to the castle that lay EAST O' THE SUN AND WEST O' THE MOON, and she answered, like the first old hag, that she knew nothing about it, except it was east o' the sun and west o' the moon.

"And thither you'll come, late or never, but you shall have the loan of my horse to my next neighbour; maybe she'll tell you all about it; and when you get there, just switch the horse under the left ear, and beg him to be off home."

And this old hag gave her the golden carding-comb; it might be she'd find some use for it, she said. So the lassie got up on the horse, and rode a far far way, and a weary time; and so at last she came to another great crag, under which sat another old hag, spinning with a golden spinning-wheel. Her, too, she asked if she knew the way to the Prince, and where the castle was that lay EAST O' THE SUN AND WEST O' THE MOON. So it was the same thing over again.

"Maybe it's you who ought to have had the Prince?" said the old hag.

Yes, it was.

But she, too, didn't know the way a bit better than the other two. "East o' the sun and west o' the moon it was," she knew—that was all.

"And thither you'll come, late or never; but I'll lend you my horse, and then I think you'd best ride to the East Wind and ask him; maybe he knows those parts, and can blow you thither. But when you get to him, you need only give the horse a switch under the left ear, and he'll trot home of himself."

And so, too, she gave her the gold spinning-wheel. "Maybe you'll find a use for it," said the old hag.

Then on she rode many many days, a weary time, before she got to the East Wind's house, but at last she did reach it, and then she asked the East Wind if he could tell her the way to the Prince who dwelt east o' the sun and west o' the moon. Yes, the East Wind had often heard tell of it, the Prince and the castle, but he couldn't tell the way, for he had never blown so far.

"But, if you will, I'll go with you to my brother the West Wind, maybe he knows, for he's much stronger. So, if you will just get on my back, I'll carry you thither."

Yes, she got on his back, and I should just think they went briskly along.

So when they got there, they went into the West Wind's house, and the East Wind said, the lassie he had brought was the one who ought to have had the Prince who lived in the castle EAST O' THE SUN AND WEST O' THE MOON; and so she had set out to seek him, and how he had come with her, and would be glad to know if the West Wind knew how to get to the castle.

"Nay," said the West Wind, "so far I've never blown; but if you will, I'll go with you to our brother the South Wind, for he's much stronger than either of us, and he has flapped his wings far and wide. Maybe he'll tell you. You can get on my back, and I'll carry you to him."

Yes! she got on his back, and so they travelled to the South Wind, and weren't so very long on the way, I should think.

When they got there, the West Wind asked him if he could tell her the way to the castle that lay EAST O' THE SUN AND WEST O' THE MOON, for it was she who ought to have had the prince who lived there.

"You don't say so! That's she, is it?" said the South Wind.

"Well, I have blustered about in most places in my time, but so far have I never blown; but if you will, I'll take you to my brother the North Wind; he is the oldest and strongest of the whole lot of us, and if he don't know where it is, you'll never find any one in the world to tell you. You can get on my back, and I'll carry you thither."

Yes! she got on his back, and away he went from his house at a fine rate. And this time, too, she wasn't long on her way.

So when they got to the North Wind's house, he was so wild and cross, cold puffs came from him a long way off.

"BLAST YOU BOTH, WHAT DO YOU WANT?" he roared out to them ever so far off, so that it struck them with an icy shiver.

"Well," said the South Wind, "you needn't be so foul-mouthed, for here I am, your brother, the South Wind, and here is the lassie who ought to have had the Prince who dwells in the castle that lies EAST O' THE SUN AND WEST O' THE MOON, and now she wants to ask you if you ever were there, and can tell her the way, for she would be so glad to find him again."

"YES, I KNOW WELL ENOUGH WHERE IT IS," said the North Wind; "once in my life I blew an aspen-leaf thither, but I was so tired I couldn't blow a puff for ever so many days after. But if you really wish to go thither, and aren't afraid to come along with me, I'll take you on my back and see if I can blow you thither."

Yes! with all her heart; she must and would get thither if it were possible in any way; and as for fear, however madly he went, she wouldn't be at all afraid.

"Very well, then," said the North Wind, "but you must sleep here to-night, for we must have the whole day before us, if we're to get thither at all."

Early next morning the North Wind woke her, and puffed himself up, and blew himself out, and made himself so stout and big, 'twas gruesome to look at him; and so off they went high up through the air, as if they would never stop till they got to the world's end.

THE SNAKE-SKIN

In Judeo-Christian tradition, the snake is an ambivalent symbol: it represents temptation, sin, transgression, and danger but also knowledge of the full range of human experiences and possibilities. In this story, collected by folklorists in nineteenth-century Hungary, an impoverished man overcomes his initial fear of a snake and chooses to bring it home as a lucky companion. This snake takes a place at the family's table and instantly brings them tremendous good fortune. The deceptiveness traditionally (and biblically!) associated with snakes is not absent from this story: it is through a series of strategic maneuvers that the snake weds a young princess, but even then his cleverness proves beneficial to all who place their trust in him. Interestingly, when the snake is revealed to be an enchanted prince and sheds the skin of the story's title, he maintains the ability to shape-shift—adopting the form of various birds when it is either convenient or amusing to do so. Many questions remain unanswered in this story: Who is this prince, and is he also a sorcerer? Why was he cursed to begin with? In this English translation by Victorian folklorists Henry Jones and Lewis Kropf, we are invited to savor a charming and artful storytelling style—and to draw on our own imaginations to fill in the gaps.

Far, very far, there was once, I do not know where, even beyond the frozen Operencian Sea, a poplar-tree, on the top of which there was a very old, tattered petticoat. In the tucks of this old petticoat I found the following tale. Whosoever listens to it will not see the kingdom of heaven.

"The Snake-Skin," in W. Henry Jones and Lewis L. Kropf, *The Folk-Tales of the Magyars* (London: Published for the Folk-Lore Society by Elliot Stock, 1889), 282–87.

There was in the world a poor man and this poor man had twelve sons. The man was so poor that sometimes he had not even enough wood to make a fire with. So he had frequently to go into the forest and would pick up there what he could find. One day, as he could not come across anything else, he was just getting ready to cut up a huge tree-stump, and, in fact, had already driven his axe into it, when an immense, dread-inspiring serpent, as big as a grown-up lad, crept out of the stump. The poor man began to ponder whether to leave it or to take it home with him; it might bring him luck or turn out a disastrous venture. At last he made up his mind that after all was said and done he would take it home with him. And so it happened, he picked up the creature and carried it home. His wife was not a little astonished at seeing him arrive with his burden, and said, "What on earth induced you, master, to bring that ugly creature home? It will frighten all the children to death."

"No fear, wife," replied the man; "they won't be afraid of it; on the contrary, they will be glad to have it to play with."

As it was just meal-time, the poor woman dished out the food and placed it on the table. The twelve children were soon seated and busily engaged with their spoons, when suddenly the serpent began to talk from underneath the table, and said, "Mother, dear, let me have some of that soup."

They were all not a little astonished at hearing a serpent talk; and the woman ladled out a plateful of soup and placed it under the bench. The snake crept to the plate and in another minute had drunk up the soup, and said: "I say, father, will you go into the larder and fetch me a loaf of bread?"

"Alas! my son," replied the poor man, "it is long—very long—since there was any bread in the larder. I was wealthy then; but now the very walls of the larder are coming down."

"Just try, father, and fetch me a loaf from there."

"What's the good of my going, when there is nothing to be found there?"

"Just go and see."

After a good deal of pressing the poor man went to the larder when—oh, joy!—he was nearly blinded by the sight of the mass of gold, silver, and other treasure; it glittered on all sides. Moreover, bacon and hams were hanging from the roof, casks filled with honey, milk, &c., standing on the floor; the bins were full of flour; in a word, there were to be seen all imaginable things to bake and roast. The poor man rushed back and fetched the family to see the miracle, and they were all astounded, but did not dare to touch anything.

Then the serpent again spoke and said: "Listen to me, mother dear. Go up to the king and ask him to give me his daughter in marriage."

"Oh, my dear son, how can you ask me to do that? You must know that the king is a great man, and he would not even listen to a pauper like myself."

"Just go and try."

So the poor woman went to the king's palace, knocked at the door, and, entering, greeted the king, and said: "May the Lord grant you a happy good day, gracious king!"

"May the Lord grant the same to you, my good woman. What have you brought? What can I do for you?"

"Hum! most gracious king, I hardly dare to speak . . . but still I will tell you . . . . My son has sent me to request your majesty to give him your youngest daughter in marriage."

"I will grant him the request, good woman, on one condition. If your son will fill with gold a sack of the size of a full-grown man, and send it here, he can have the princess at any minute."

The poor woman was greatly pleased at hearing this; returned home and delivered the message.

"That can easily be done, dear mother. Let's have a wagon, and the king shall have the gold to a grain."

And so it happened. They borrowed a wagon of the king, the serpent filled a sack of the required size full of gold, and put a heap of gold and diamonds loose in the wagon besides. The king was not a little astonished, and exclaimed, "Well! upon my word, although I am a king I do not possess so much gold as this lad." And the princess was accordingly given away.

It happened that the two elder princesses were also to be married shortly, and orders were issued by the king that the wedding of his youngest daughter should take place at the same time. The state carriage was therefore wheeled out of the shed, six fine horses were put to it, the youngest princess sat in it and drove straight to the poor man's cottage to fetch her bridegroom. But the poor girl very nearly jumped out of the coach when she saw the snake approaching. But the snake tried to allay her fears and said, "Don't shrink from me, I am your bridegroom," and with this crept into the carriage. The bride—poor thing, what could she do?—put her arm round the snake and covered him with her shawl, as she did not wish to let the whole town know her misfortune. Then they drove to church. The priest threw up his arms in amazement when he saw the bridegroom approach the altar. From church they drove to the castle. There kings, princes, dukes, barons, and deputy-lieutenants of the counties were assembled at the festival and enjoying themselves; they were all dancing their legs off in true Magyar style, and very nearly kicked out the sides of the dancing-room, when suddenly the youngest princess entered, followed by her bridegroom, who crept everywhere after her. The king upon seeing this grew very angry, and exclaimed, "Get out of my sight! A girl who will marry such a husband does not deserve to stay under the same roof with me, and I will take care that you two do not remain here. Body-guards, conduct this woman with her snake-husband down into the poultry-yard, and lock them up in the darkest poultry-house among the geese. Let them stay there, and don't allow them to come here to shock my guests with their presence."

And so it happened. The poor couple were locked up with the geese; there they were left crying and weeping, and lived in great sorrow until the day when the curse expired, and the snake—who was a bewitched prince—became a very handsome young man, whose very hair was of pure gold. And, as you may imagine, great was the bride's joy when she saw the change.

"I say, love," spoke her prince, "I will go home to my father's and fetch some clothes and other things; in the meantime, stay here; don't be afraid. I shall be back here long without fail."

Then the prince shook himself and became a white pigeon, and flew away. Having arrived at his father's place he said to his parent, "My dear

father, let me have back my former horse, my saddle, sword, gun, and all my other goods and chattels. The power of the curse has now passed away, and I have taken a wife to myself."

"The horse is in the stables, my son, and all your other things are up in the loft."

The prince led out his horse, fetched down his things from the loft, put on his rich uniform all glittering with gold, mounted his charger, and flew up into the air. He was yet at a good distance from the castle where the festivities were still going on, when all the loveliest princesses turned out and crowded the balconies to see who the great swell was whom they saw coming. He did not pass under the crossbeam of the gate, but flew over it like a bird. He tied his charger to a tree in the yard, and then entered the castle and walked among the dancers. The dance was immediately stopped, everybody gazed upon him and admired him, and tried to get into his favour. For amusement several of the guests did various tricks; at last his turn came, and by Jove! he did show them things that made the guests open their mouths and eyes in astonishment. He could transform himself into a wild duck, a pigeon, a quail, and so on, into anything one could conceive of.

After the conjuring was over he went into the poultry-yard to fetch his bride. He made her a hundred times prettier than she already was, and dressed her up in rich garments of pure silver and gold. The assembled guests were very sorry that the handsome youth in rich attire, who had shown them such amusing and clever tricks, had so soon left them.

All at once the king remembered the newly-married couple and thought he would go to see what the young folks were doing in the poultry-yard. He sent down a few of his friends, who were nearly overpowered by the shine and glitter on looking into the poultry-house. They at once unlocked the door, and led the bride and bridegroom into their royal father's presence. When they entered the castle, everyone was struck with wonder at discovering that the bridegroom was no one else than the youth who had amused them shortly before.

Then the bridegroom walked up to the king and said: "Gracious majesty, my father and king, for the past twelve years I lay under a curse and was compelled to wear a serpent's skin. When I entered, not long ago, your castle in my former plight, I was the laughing-stock of everybody, all present mocked me. But now, as my time of curse has passed, let me see the man who can put himself against me."

"There is, indeed, nobody, no man living," replied the king.

The bridegroom then led off his bride to the dance, and celebrated such a fine wedding, that it was talked of over seven countries.

PRINCE CHÉRI

Jeanne-Marie Leprince de Beaumont was a French writer working as a governess in England when she published her best-known fairy tale "Beauty and the Beast" (1757). Less well known today is de Beaumont's story "Prince Chéri," which appeared in the same collection and even takes up a similar theme of animal-human relationships. The story certainly begins on a remarkably modern note: the fairy Candid punishes Prince Chéri for kicking a dog, arguing that people who have power over others, whether human or animal, do not have the right to abuse that power. In this complex tale, Chéri must shape-shift several times before he gains the self-knowledge needed to be crowned king. The prince progresses through the animal kingdom learning different lessons as he takes the form of various creatures, and he is also transformed into a monstrous hybrid of animal parts, each one representing his faults of temperament, behavior, and morality. When de Beaumont wrote this tale in the mid-eighteenth century, European thinkers were engaged in debates about animal rights and connected these concerns to ideas about human rights and dignity—the great tenets of modern democracy. By linking the treatment of animals to the treatment of people, including the ways in which sovereigns rule over nations, de Beaumont's tale becomes a commentary on the political abuse of power. Does the fairy Candid still have something to teach us today?

There was once upon a time so excellent a monarch that his subjects called him King Good. One day, when he was hunting, a little white rabbit which the dogs were about to kill, jumped into his arms. The King caressed the little rabbit, and said, "As it has put itself under my protection,

Jeanne-Marie Leprince de Beaumont, "Prince Chéri" (1757), in *Four and Twenty Fairy Tales Selected from Those of Perrault and Other Popular Writers,* translated by J. R. Planché (London: G. Routledge, 1858), 484–93.

I will not allow any harm to be done to it." He carried the little rabbit into his palace and gave it a pretty little house and nice herbs to eat. At night, when he was alone in his chamber, a beautiful lady appeared before him; she was arrayed neither in gold nor in silver, but her robe was white as snow, and her head-dress consisted simply of a crown of white roses. The good King was much surprised to see this lady, as his door was locked, and he knew not how she had entered. She said to him, "I am the Fairy Candid; I passed through the wood as you were hunting, and I wished to ascertain if you were as good as everybody said you were. For that purpose I took the form of a little rabbit, and I saved myself by jumping into your arms; for I know that those who have pity for animals have more still for men; and if you had refused me your assistance I should have thought you wicked. I come to thank you for the kindness you have shown me, and to assure you I shall always be your friend. You have only to ask me for anything you wish, I promise to grant it."

"Madam," said the good King, "as you are a Fairy, you ought to know all I wish for. I have but one son, whom I love exceedingly, and on that account they have named him Prince Chéri; if you have any affection for me, become the friend of my son." "With all my heart," said the Fairy; "I can make your son the handsomest Prince in the world, or the richest, or the most powerful; choose which you wish him to be." "I desire none of those things for my son," said the good King; "but I shall be much obliged if you will make him the best of all Princes. What will it profit him to be handsome, rich, to have all the kingdoms of the world, if he should be wicked? You know well he would be miserable, and that nothing but virtue can make him happy." "You are quite right," said Candid; "but it is not in my power to make the Prince Chéri a good man in spite of himself; he must himself endeavour to become virtuous. All I can promise you is to give him good advice, to point out to him his faults, and to punish him if he will not correct them and punish himself."

The good King was quite content with this promise, and died a short time afterwards. Prince Chéri wept much for his father, for he loved him with all his heart, and he would have given all his kingdoms, his gold, and his silver, to have saved him, if such things had power to change the will of fate. Two years after the death of the good King, Chéri being in bed, Candid appeared to him. "I promised your father," said she to him, "to be your friend; and, to keep my word, I come to make you a present." At the same time she placed on the finger of Chéri a little gold ring, and said to him, "Keep this ring carefully—it is more precious than diamonds. Every time you commit a bad action it will prick your finger; but if in spite of this pricking you persist in the evil deed, you will lose my friendship, and I shall become your enemy."

Candid disappeared as she uttered these words, and left Chéri much astonished. For some time his conduct was so faultless that the ring did not prick him at all, and this gave him so much gratification, that his subjects added to his name Chéri, or Beloved, that of Heureux, or Happy. One day he went out hunting, and caught nothing, which put him in a bad humour. It appeared to him, then, that the ring pressed his finger a little; but as it did not prick him he paid no great attention to it. On entering his apartment, however, his little dog Bibi came jumping about him affectionately, when he said, "Get thee gone, I am not in a humour to receive thy caresses!" The poor little dog, who did not understand him, pulled at his coat, to oblige him at least to look at him. This irritated Chéri, and he gave him a violent kick. In a moment the ring pricked him, as if it had been a pin; he was much astonished, and seated himself, quite ashamed, in a corner of the room. "I think the Fairy mocks me," said he to himself. "What great evil have I done in kicking an animal which worried me? Of what use is it to be master of a great empire if I may not chastise my own dog?" "I do not mock you," said a voice which replied to the thoughts of Chéri. "You have committed three faults instead of one. You have been in an ill-humour because you did not like to be disappointed, and because you believe both beasts and men were only made to obey you. You put yourself in a passion, which is very wrong, and, lastly, you have been cruel to a poor animal that did not deserve to be ill-treated. I know you are much superior to a dog; but if it were a reasonable thing, and permissible for the great to ill-treat those who are beneath them, I would at this moment beat you—kill you, for a Fairy is stronger than a man. The advantage of being master of a great empire is not to be able to do all the harm that you may wish, but all the good that you can." Chéri confessed his fault, and promised to correct it; but he did not keep his word. He had been reared by a foolish nurse, who bad spoilt him when he was little. If he wanted anything he had only to cry, pout, and stamp his foot, and this woman gave him all he wished for; and this had made him wilful. She had told him also, from morning to night, that he would be King someday, and that kings were very happy, because everybody must obey them, and treat them with great respect, and that no one could prevent their doing whatever they pleased.

When Chéri grew up, and was capable of reasoning, he soon learnt that there was nothing so odious as to be proud, vain, and obstinate. He made some efforts to correct himself, but he had unfortunately contracted all three defects; and a bad habit is very difficult to eradicate. It was not that he had naturally a bad heart: he wept with annoyance when he had committed a fault, and said, "How unfortunate am I in having to fight thus all my days against my pride and my temper! If they had corrected me when I was young, I should not now have had so much trouble." His ring pricked him very often. Sometimes he stopped immediately, at others he persisted in his ill-behaviour; and what was very singular was, that it pricked him very slightly for a light offence, but when he did anything really wicked, it would make the blood spurt from his finger. At length he grew impatient at this, and wishing to sin at his ease, he threw away his ring. He thought himself the happiest of men when he was released from its pricking. He abandoned himself to all the follies which entered his head, till at length he became quite wicked, and nobody could bear him.

One day that Chéri was out walking he saw a young maiden so beautiful, that he determined to marry her. She was called Zélie, and she was as good as she was pretty. Chéri imagined that Zélie would be most happy to become a great Queen; but the girl told him, with much firmness, "Sire, I am only a shepherdess; I have no fortune; but in spite of that, I will not marry you." "Am I displeasing to you?" asked Chéri, a little offended. "No, Prince," replied Zélie; "I think you are very handsome; but what would be the advantage to me of your beauty, your riches, the fine clothes and magnificent carriages which you would give me, if the bad actions I should daily see you commit forced me to despise and hate you?"

Chéri became enraged with Zélie, and ordered his officers to carry her by force to his palace. He brooded all day long over the contempt with which this girl had treated him; but as he loved her, he could not make up his mind to harm her. Amongst the favourites of Chéri was his foster-brother, whom he had made his confidant. This man, whose inclinations were as low as his birth, flattered the passions of his master, and gave him very bad advice. When he saw Chéri so sad, he asked the cause of his grief. The Prince having replied that he could not bear the contempt of Zélie, and that he had determined to correct himself of his faults, because he must be virtuous to please her, this wicked man said, "You are very good to give yourself so much trouble for a little girl. If I were in your place, I would force her to obey me. Remember that you are King, and that it would be a shame for you to submit to the will of a shepherdess who should be only too happy to be amongst your slaves. Make her fast on bread and water; put her in prison; and if she continue to refuse to marry you, let her die by torture, in order to teach others to yield to your wishes. You will be disgraced if it be known that a simple girl resists your pleasure, and all your subjects will forget that they are placed in this world only to serve you." "But," said Chéri, "shall I not be disgraced if I put to death an innocent girl? For in fact Zélie is guilty of no crime." "No one is innocent who refuses to obey your commands," replied the confidant. "But suppose you do commit an injustice, it is better to be accused of that than to let it be known that it is permitted to be wanting in respect for you or to contradict you."

The courtier knew Chéri's weak point; and the fear of seeing his authority diminished made such an impression on the King, that he stifled the good impulse which had given him the wish to correct himself. He resolved to go the same evening into the chamber of the shepherdess, and to ill-treat her if she still refused to marry him.

The foster-brother of Chéri, who feared some good change in him, assembled three young lords as wicked as himself to carouse with the King. They supped together; and the courtiers took care to cloud the reason of the poor Prince, by making him drink deep. During the repast they excited his anger against Zélie, and made him so ashamed of the tenderness he had shown for her, that he rose like a madman, swearing that he would make her obey him, or sell her the next day as a slave.

Chéri having entered the chamber in which the girl had been shut up, was surprised not to find her there, for he had the key in his pocket. He was in a frightful rage, and swore to be avenged on those whom he should suspect of having aided her to escape. His confidants hearing him speak thus, resolved to profit by his anger to rid themselves of a nobleman who had been Chéri's governor. This worthy man had occasionally taken the liberty of pointing out to the King his faults, for he loved him as though he had been his own son. At first Chéri had thanked him, but at length he grew impatient at being contradicted, and then began to think it was only from a spirit of opposition that his governor found fault with him, whilst everyone else praised him. He ordered him, therefore, to retire from Court; but, notwithstanding this order, he admitted now and then that he was an honest man; that he no longer loved him, but that he esteemed him in spite of himself. The favourites were always in dread of the King recalling the governor, and they now imagined they had found a favourable opportunity of getting rid of him altogether. They represented to the King that Suliman (such was the name of the worthy man) had boasted that he would set Zélie at liberty. They bribed three men, who deposed that they had overheard Suliman speak to this effect; and the Prince, transported with anger, commanded his foster-brother to send a guard to bring the governor to him fettered like a criminal.

After having given these orders, Chéri retired to his room; but hardly had he entered it, when the ground trembled, he heard a tremendous clap of thunder, and Candid appeared before him. "I promised your father," said she to him, in a severe tone, "to give you advice, and to punish you if you refused to follow it. You have scorned that advice; you have retained but the form of a man; your crimes have changed you into a monster, the horror of heaven and earth. It is time I should fulfil my promise by punishing you. I condemn you to become like the beasts whose inclinations you already copy. You have resembled the lion in your rage, the wolf in your gluttony, the serpent by wounding him who has been your second father, and the bull by your brutality. You shall bear in your new form the trace of all these animals."

Hardly had she finished these words before Chéri saw with horror he was the monster she described. He had the head of a lion, the horns of a bull, the feet of a wolf, and the tail of a viper. At the same time he found himself in a great forest, on the brink of a fountain wherein he saw his horrible form reflected, and heard a voice, which said, "Consider attentively the state to which thy crimes have reduced thee. Thy mind is become a thousand times more frightful than thy body." Chéri recognised the voice of Candid, and in his fury he turned to throw himself on her, and, if it had been possible, to devour her; but he saw no one, and the same voice said to him, "I mock thy impotent fury, and will humble thy pride by placing thee under the power of thine own subjects."

Chéri thought that by flying from this fountain he should escape from much of his vexation, as he should no longer have his ugliness and deformity before his eyes: he rushed therefore into the wood; but hardly had he gone a few steps, when he fell into a hole which had been made to catch a bear, and immediately the hunters, who had climbed the trees to watch for their prey, descended, and having secured him with chains, led him towards the capital city of his kingdom.

On the way, instead of perceiving that he had drawn on himself this chastisement by his own fault, he cursed the Fairy, gnawed his chains, and gave himself up to his rage. As he approached the city to which they were conducting him, he observed great rejoicing going on; and the hunters having asked what had happened, were told that Prince Chéri, who had had no pleasure but in tormenting his people, had been destroyed in his chamber by a thunderbolt, for so they imagined. "The gods," said they, "could no longer support the excess of his wickedness, and have thus ridden the world of him. Four lords, accomplices of his crimes, thought to profit by the event, and to divide his kingdom amongst them; but the people who knew that it was their evil counsel which had corrupted the King, tore them to pieces, and have offered the crown to Suliman, whom the wicked Chéri had wished to put to death. This worthy Lord has just been crowned, and we celebrate this day as that of the deliverance of the kingdom; for Suliman is virtuous, and will restore to us peace and prosperity."

Chéri groaned with rage at hearing this discourse; but it was far worse when he arrived in the Great Square before the Palace. He saw Suliman on a superb throne, and heard the people wish him a long life, to repair all the evils which his predecessor had committed. Suliman made a sign with his hand to request silence, and said to the crowd: "I have accepted the crown which you offered me, but only to preserve it for Prince Chéri; he is not dead, as you believe. A Fairy has revealed this to me, and perhaps someday you will see him again as virtuous as he was in his youth. Alas!" continued he, shedding tears, "flatterers ruined him. I knew his heart, it was formed for virtue; and but for the poisonous discourse of those who surrounded him, he would have been a father to you. Detest his vices, but pity him, and let us all pray the gods to restore him to us. As for me, I should esteem myself too happy to bathe this throne with my blood, if I could see him ascend it again with those good dispositions which would make him fill it worthily."

The words of Suliman went to the heart of Chéri. He found then how sincere had been the attachment and fidelity of this excellent man, and for the first time reproached himself for his wickedness. Hardly had he listened to this good impulse than he felt the rage which had animated him subdued, he reflected on the crimes he had committed, and confessed he had not been punished as severely as he had deserved. He ceased to struggle in his iron cage, and became mild as a lamb. They placed him in a large menagerie, where they kept all sorts of monsters and wild beasts, and chained him up with the rest.

Chéri then came to the resolution of beginning to amend of his faults, by showing obedience to the man who kept him. This man was very brutal when he was in an ill-temper. Although the Monster was very docile, he beat him without rhyme or reason. One day that this man was asleep, a tiger that had broken his chain threw himself upon him to devour him; at first Chéri felt an emotion of joy at seeing himself about to be delivered from his persecutor, but immediately after he condemned this feeling and wished himself at liberty. "I would," said he, "render good for evil by saving the life of this unhappy man." Hardly had be formed the wish, than he saw his iron cage open, he threw himself before the man, who was now awake and defending himself from the tiger. The Keeper thought himself lost when he saw the Monster; but his fear was soon turned into joy—the benevolent Monster sprang upon the tiger, strangled him, and then laid himself down at the feet of him whom he had saved. The man, penetrated by gratitude, was about to stoop to caress the Monster which had rendered him so great a service, when he heard a voice which said, "A good action never goes without its reward," and at the same moment he saw only a pretty dog at his feet. Chéri, charmed at this metamorphosis, bestowed a thousand caresses on his Keeper, who took him in his arms and carried him to the King, to whom he related this marvellous story. The Queen desired to have the dog; and Chéri would have been very happy in his new condition had he been able to forget that he was once a man and a monarch. The Queen loaded him with caresses; but fearing that he would grow larger, she consulted her physicians, who told her that she must give him no food but bread, and only a moderate quantity of that. Poor Chéri was dying of hunger half the day, but he was obliged to have patience.

One morning that they brought him his little roll for his breakfast, he had a fancy to go and eat it in the garden of the Palace. He took it in his mouth, and walked towards a canal which he knew was a short distance off; but he could nowhere find it, and in its place he saw a large mansion, the exterior of which blazed with gold and precious stones. He observed in it an immense number of persons of both sexes magnificently dressed: they sang and danced, and fared sumptuously within the building; but all those who came out of it were pale, thin, covered with wounds, and nearly naked, for their clothes were torn into shreds. Some fell dead as they issued from it without having strength to drag themselves a step further; others proceeded with great difficulty; whilst some remained lying on the ground dying of hunger and begging a morsel of bread from those who entered the house, but who did not vouchsafe a look at them. Chéri approached a young girl who was trying to tear up some grass to eat; touched with compassion, the Prince said to himself, "I have a good appetite, but I shall not die of hunger if I wait till dinner-time and sacrifice my breakfast to this poor creature; perhaps I shall save her life." He resolved to act on this good impulse, and placed his bread in the hand of the girl, who put it to her mouth with avidity. She soon appeared quite restored by it; and Chéri, transported with joy at having so opportunely come to her relief, was about to return to the Palace when he heard loud cries. It was Zélie in the hands of four men, who dragged her towards the mansion, which they forced her to enter. Chéri then regretted his form of a monster, which would have afforded him the means of rescuing Zélie; but a poor little dog as he was, he could only bark at the ravishers and strive to follow them. They drove him away by kicks; but he resolved not to quit the spot, and find out what had become of Zélie. He reproached himself for the misfortunes of this beautiful girl. "Alas!" said he to himself, "I am indignant with those who have carried her off. Have I not committed the same crime myself? and if the justice of the gods had not frustrated my attempt, should I not have treated her with the same barbarity?"

The reflections of Chéri were interrupted by a noise which he heard above his head. He saw a window open; and his joy was extreme when he perceived Zélie, who threw from this window a plateful of meat so well dressed that it made him hungry to see it. The window was shut again immediately; and Chéri, who had not eaten all day, was about to devour the meat, when the young girl to whom he had given the bread uttered a cry, and having taken him in her arms, "Poor little animal," said she, "do not touch that food; this house is the Palace of Voluptuousness; all who come out of it are poisoned." At the same moment Chéri heard a voice which said, "Thou seest a good action never remains unrecompensed"; and immediately he was changed into a beautiful little white pigeon. He remembered that this colour was the favourite one of Candid, and began to hope that she might at length restore him to her good graces. He was desirous of rejoining Zélie; and rising in the air, flew all round the palace, and found with joy one window open; but in vain did he traverse all the building—he could not find Zélie. In despair at her loss, he resolved not to rest till he should meet with her. He flew for several days, and having entered a desert, observed a cavern, which he approached. How great was his delight! Zélie was seated there by the side of a venerable hermit, and sharing with him a frugal repast. Chéri, transported with joy, flew on to the shoulder of the lovely shepherdess, and expressed by his caresses the pleasure he felt at seeing her. Zélie, charmed with the gentleness of the little creature, stroked it gently with her hand, and although she thought it could not understand her, she told it that she accepted the gift it made her of itself, and that she would always love it. "What have you done, Zélie?" said the hermit. "You have plighted your faith." "Yes, charming shepherdess," said Chéri to her, who resumed at this moment his natural form, "the termination of my metamorphosis was dependent on your consent to our union. You have promised always to love me, confirm my happiness, or I shall hasten and implore the Fairy Candid, my protectress, to restore me to the form under which I have had the happiness of pleasing you." "You need not fear her inconstancy," said Candid, who, quitting the form of the hermit under which she had been concealed, appeared before them in her proper person. "Zélie loved you from the first moment she saw you; but your vices compelled her to conceal the passion with which you had inspired her. The change in your heart leaves her at liberty to show her affection for you. You will live happily, because your union will be founded on virtue."

Chéri and Zélie threw themselves at the feet of Candid. The Prince was never tired of thanking her for her goodness, and Zélie, enchanted to find that the Prince detested his former evil ways, confirmed to him the Fairy's avowal of her affection. "Rise, my children," said the Fairy to them, "I will transport you to your Palace, and restore to Chéri a crown of which his vices had rendered him unworthy." Hardly had she finished speaking when they found themselves in the chamber of Suliman, who, charmed to see his dear master once more become virtuous, abdicated the throne, and remained the most faithful of his subject. Chéri reigned for a long period with Zélie; and it is said that he applied himself so well to his duties, that the ring, which he again wore, never once pricked his finger severely enough to draw a single drop of blood.

THE MAIDEN AND THE FISH

A fish out of water asks to be thrown into a well—this is logical enough as a premise for a tale. But in this Portuguese story, the fish rules over a sumptuous underwater world and wants his human savoir, a downtrodden young girl charmed by the fish's beauty, to follow him right in. When she does, she lives a Cinderella fantasy. Richly attired beyond her means, she attends a ball where she dazzles her unsuspecting sisters with her beauty and then loses a slipper on her way out. As the story follows the plot of "Cinderella," first written in French by Charles Perrault in the seventeenth century, we might wonder about how the intrigue of the prince cursed into the form of a fish alters our perception of the Cinderella tale. A girl dubbed "Hearth-Cat" by her sisters would appear to be a very unlikely savior figure for a fish, but in this tale our heroine is as essential to the prince's good fortune as he is to hers. Finally the insult-hurling sisters are punished for their cruelty and, bitter and jealous, begin "to throw all manner of filth out of their mouths." "The Maiden and the Fish" is among five hundred stories collected from oral storytellers across Portugal by the folklorist and historian Consiglieri Pedroso. The points of similarity and contrast between this tale and more familiar stories demonstrate the ways in which storytellers and literary authors alike draw creatively from rich wells of cultural material.

Once there was a widower who had three daughters. The two eldest thought of nothing but dress and finery, and going to amusements, or sitting at the

"The Maiden and the Fish," translated by Miss Henriqueta Monteiro, in Consiglieri Pedroso, *Portuguese Folk-Tales*, Folk Lore Society Publications, Vol. 9 (New York: Folk Lore Society Publications, 1882), 97–99.

window doing nothing; whilst the youngest occupied herself with the household management, and was fond of assisting the servant in the kitchen, and for which reason her sisters called her the "Hearth-Cat." One day the father caught a fish and brought it home alive, and as the youngest daughter was the one who occupied herself in cooking, and was besides his favourite child, he gave her the fish to prepare for their supper. As the fish was alive, and she took a great liking to it on account of its pretty yellow colour, she placed it in a large pan with water, and begged her father to allow her to keep it for herself, and not kill it. As soon as the father consented to her keeping it, she at once took it to her own room and gave it plenty of water to swim in; and when the sisters saw what had been done with the fish they began to cry out and complain that, for the sake of pleasing the "Hearth-Cat," they were to be deprived of eating that excellent fish.

At night, when the little maiden had already laid herself down to sleep, the fish began to say to her, "Oh! maiden, throw me into the well! Oh! maiden, throw me into the well!" The fish repeated this so often and so imploringly that at length she rose and threw the fish into the well. The following day she took a walk in the garden to try and see the fish, as she quite yearned to have a look at it once more; and as she drew close to the well she heard a voice inside which said: "Oh! maiden, come into the well! Oh! maiden, come into the well!" She ran away with fear; but on the following day, when the sisters were gone to the festival, the maiden again approached the border of the well, and she heard once more the same voice calling for her, and, impelled by it, she went into the well; and she had hardly reached the bottom when the fish appeared to her, and, laying hold of her hand, he conducted her to a palace of gold and precious stones, and said to her: "Go into that chamber and attire yourself in the best and most elegant robe you find there, and put on a pair of gold slippers which are ready for you, as you will see, for I mean you to go to the same festival as your sisters are gone to. You will proceed to it in a splendid state carriage which you will find ready for you at the door when you leave this palace. At the conclusion of the festival be careful to take your departure before your sisters do, and return here to take off your robes, for I promise you that a time is in store for you when you will be very happy indeed." When the maiden had put on garments worked in gold and precious stones of very great value, she came out of the well, and on reaching the palace door she found a splendid carriage ready for her. She stepped in and proceeded to the festival. When she entered the edifice every one there was in admiration, and wondered from whence had come such a lovely, comely maiden with such rich robes. She left the edifice without loss of time the very moment that the festival was concluded; but in her hurry to get out she lost one of her slippers, and the king, who was following close behind her, picked it up, and ordered an edict to be issued that he would marry the maiden to whom that slipper belonged. When she reached home she went into the well at once to take off her rich garments, and when she left the enchanted palace the fish told her to return in the evening, for he wished to ask her something. The maiden promised to comply with his wish, and departed.

When her sisters returned home she was seen busy in the kitchen, and they gave her a glowing account of the beautiful lady they had seen at the feast, who had on such rich robes full of gold ornaments and precious stones such as they had never seen before in their lives, and how this fair and lovely maiden had dropped one of her dainty slippers in her hurry to leave the edifice, which the king had picked up, and now signified his intention of marrying the maiden to whom it belonged. They told her that such being the state of affairs, they would go to the palace to try the slipper, and were certain that it would fit one of them, who would then be made a queen! and then would she give the "Hearth-Cat" a new dress. The moment the sisters left for the palace the maiden went to the well to see the fish, who said to her the moment he saw her, "Oh, maiden! will you marry me?" The maiden replied, "I cannot possibly marry a fish!" but he so entreated her, and urged his suit so ardently, that she at last consented. That very instant the fish was transformed into a man, who said to her, "Know, then, that I am a prince who was enchanted here, and am the son of the sovereign who governs these realms. I know that my father has published an edict, ordering all the maidens of his kingdom to repair to the palace and try on the slipper which you dropped to-day on coming away from the feast; go, therefore, there yourself, and when the king tells you that you must marry him, inform him that you are already engaged to the prince, his son, who was enchanted, for his majesty will then send for me on hearing this." The maiden left the well, and shortly after her sisters returned from the palace looking very downcast and disappointed because the slipper after all did not fit them. The maiden then hinted to them that she also thought of repairing to the palace, to try on the slipper in case it should fit her. The sisters indignantly said: "Just see what airs the 'Hearth-Cat' is putting on, and is not ashamed of herself. Go, and show your tiny, dainty foot! go." The maiden went to the palace, nevertheless; and the sentinels, seeing her so shabbily dressed, would not let her pass; but the king, who just happened to be at the window, ordered them to let her enter. He had hardly given her the tiny slipper to try on when his majesty remained struck with wonder to see how soon she drew it on, and how beautifully the slipper fitted her, and he that moment told her that he would make her his queen. The maiden, however, very respectfully signified to him that it could not be, as she was already engaged to be the bride of his majesty's son, the prince who had been spell-bound so long. The king, on hearing her, could scarcely contain his delight to think that he would soon see his son again, disenchanted as he was now. He immediately sent a retinue of the grandees of the realm to bring his son out of the well, and he married him to the beautiful maiden. There were great rejoicings and much feasting in honour of the occasion; and the sisters of the "Hearth-Cat," filled with jealousy and bitterness at the sudden turn of affairs, were punished, and commenced to throw all manner of filth out of their mouths. The "Hearth-Cat" remained in the palace the bride of the prince, who afterwards succeeded to the throne, and became king.

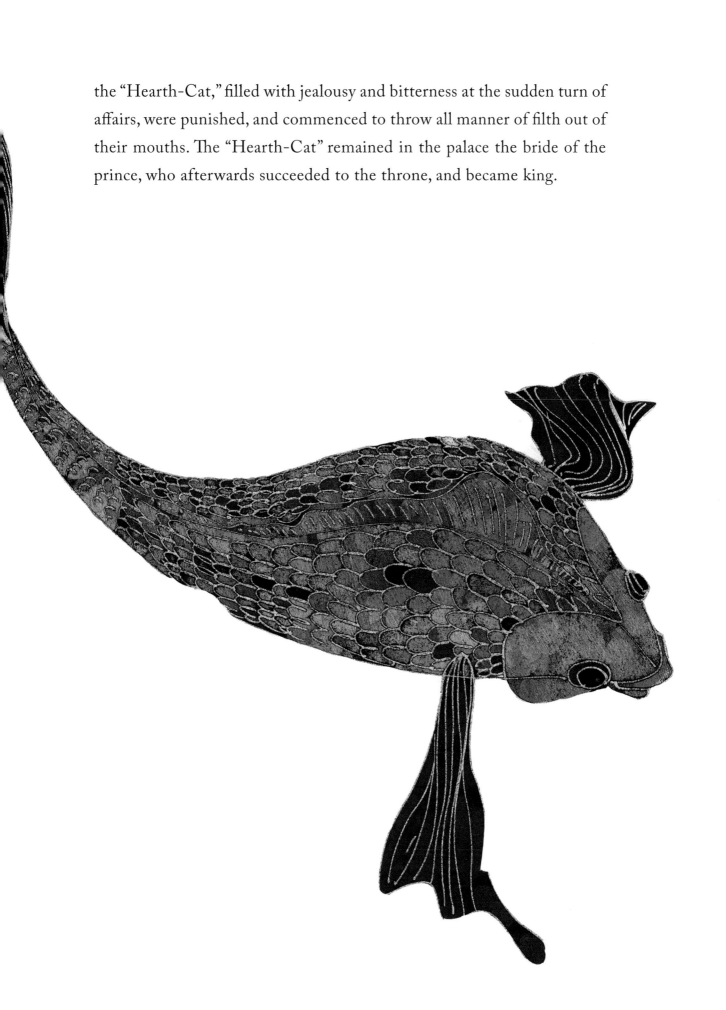

ABOUT THE EDITORS

Jennifer Schacker is associate professor of English at the University of Guelph and author of *National Dreams: The Remaking of Fairy Tales in Nineteenth-Century England.*

Christine A. Jones is associate professor of French at the University of Utah and author of *Shapely Bodies: The Image of Porcelain in Eighteenth-Century France.* Jones and Schacker are longtime collaborators and co-editors of *Marvelous Transformations: An Anthology of Fairy Tales and Contemporary Critical Perspectives.*

ABOUT THE ILLUSTRATOR

Lina Kusaite is an illustrator, designer, and art/life coach based in Brussels, Belgium. Her work has appeared in a wide range of international publications, computer games, and exhibitions, and was selected for display in Times Square as part of the see.me 2014 "seemetakeover" event. Kusaite's website is www.behance.net/cocooncharacters.